Table of Contents

Gary Doherty

8 Hours / 8 Visits

I look down at the tag hanging around my neck. It identifies me as a guardian from the State of Illinois. I'd prefer a new picture but the bureaucracy of obtaining one from the state makes me settle for what I have. I wait in silence.

I walk into the elevator and watch a five-year-old push the number 2 button with guarded supervision from Mom. She looks up with prideful cherub eyes. I give a thumb's up and a smile. The door opens and I head toward *Covenant Hospital's Intensive Care Unit*.

On the unit Dr. T says, "Pat needs her code status changed to *Do Not Resuscitate*. We may consider a hospice referral as well." I explain the *Office of State Guardian DNR* policy, and arrange to have the forms sent from my office.

I look in on 'Pat'. She has lost the magical zeal that most Down Syndrome people own. She's like the rest of the sick folk up and down the hallway. The bi-pap machine whispers air into her soul. No family has chosen to hang on to 'Pat'. No one to sit and hold her hand or dab a cold washcloth on her forehead.

I speak into her ear, sign consent for treatment, and leave the unit.

I drive to *Gibson City nursing home* where I serve as guardian for a couple married over sixty years. Mrs. passed away three weeks ago. She gave some of her body to science. The rest of her cremains are in a box on a shelf in the administrator's office.

Mr. asks me, "Where is Lottie?"

I patiently explain, "Lottie's heart gave up. She's in Heaven."

He stares into my face with a look of shock and grief. I get on my hands and knees and look through a box of their *papers* to find a picture of Lottie.

He asks again, "Where is Lottie?"

I explain again, "Lottie is in heaven." I wonder at the cruelty of *this dementia* that forces Mr. to learn and react to the tragedy dozens of times a day.

There is no picture.

Mr. talks of having killed someone when he was in the Korean War. I contact the bank that manages their money. They have some pictures! They will mail them to the nursing home.

I ask the social service worker to hang a picture of Lottie in Mr.'s room with her birth and death dates on the bottom. Who knows if it will help this man?

I tell him, "You are a good man. You were a wonderful husband to Lottie."

I leave the room.

The administrator wants to talk to me. They have a resident who is being financially exploited by a family member. I give her the names of agencies that might help.

I drive to Casey's convenience store and buy a banana and diet Coke. I'm tempted by slices of pizza rotating in a warming oven. My back is sweaty, it's the price of being a *big guy*.

Next stop, Paxton. I park under the shade of an Elm on Maple Street and enter a large elderly house that is officially titled *Community Integrated Living Arrangement*. Five women sit at a table. Their jobs are designed to make the lives of the developmentally disabled a bit more pleasant.

I am here for Rita's annual meeting; to review the objectives of last year's *Individual Service Plan,* and create an outline for next year.

It's a process so different from anything a *normal* person would ever encounter.

But it is the best they've come up with for now.

I kid Rita that all my official paperwork indicates her name is Bernice.

She giggles.

Rita has had a great year.

Her family abandoned her when she was eighteen years old at a local homeless shelter. She has no one except *group home night staff* to call if she needs someone at 3 a.m. I admire how she deals with it.

She was so angry at her meetings ten years ago that we had to quit and restart. She used profanity as her fists. Now, she is a mature calm woman who averages only two of these behaviors a month. They track these things.

Bonnie, another person on my caseload who lives in the same house as Rita, wants to talk to me. Before our agency became her adult guardian, the *Department of Children and Family Services* served her.

Bonnie has lived in 30 different foster or residential homes within the last 10 years. "Can I get a SafeLink cell phone?" she asks me now. "They're free."

I read over the application and apparently *it is free*. I look up, "OK." She has a brand-new smile on her twenty-four-year-old face.

She expected a "No."

Bonnie is allowed one call a day to her biological parents. Mom and Dad are divorced. Each parent calls Bonnie to vent about how angry they are at their former spouse.

3

But the calls are what Bonnie looks forward to.

It is *normal* to talk to your family.

I drive to another nursing home. I moved Brent to this place a week ago. He was asked to leave the previous nursing home because he was caught smoking indoors.

He also had booze snuck into the facility in a Mountain Dew can.

And occasionally stored other resident's medications in his dresser drawer.

He is younger than my fifty-four years of age. He was never diagnosed with mental illness, but I've witnessed traits of borderline personality disorder.

Brent has already taken advantage of the *no smoking program* in his new home. His seventy-seven-year-old Mom sent him $75 dollars when he first moved in.

The money is spent.

He told his Mom the facility never got her check.

He tells the facility she is sending another one.

I leave the cigarette battle to be waged between them.

Before being institutionalized, Brent lived in his Mom's basement.

He drank vodka.

He drank himself into a sixty-day catatonic coma.

He pleads with his Mom to return to that basement.

I am the mean guardian who says, "No!"

I get into the *state car* and listen to the radio. Kankakee is next on my agenda. Wise men orate about the White Sox and Cubs scores. They tell me who the Bulls should draft. I go to a McDonald's, call the office, and ask the managing attorney, Bill, for the name of the *new guy* he asked me to visit at *Riverside Medical Center*.

There will be no visit.

Bill forgot to tell me the *new guy* died early this morning.

Bill asks, "Can you visit another *new guy*? He's on intensive care at *St. Mary's Hospital?"*

"Yes."

I listen to my voice mails:

1. Bob from a group home. "We've lost our funding. We can't accept your guy for placement." The *guy* was scheduled to move next week. This news will break his heart. My heart breaks for him.

2. A speech pathologist from a nursing home, "Lucy has failed her swallowing evaluation. Do you want her to have a feeding tube in her tummy or not?"

3. Two voicemails about Robert, "Robert has had two falls in two days with no injuries." But how can I be sure a man with *end stage dementia* is OK, just because he says he's alright?

4. Tim from the office, "I'm giving verbal consent for a reduction of Frieda's Risperdal from 3mg at night to 2.75mg."

5. Art, the owner of a rural cemetery, "I can't find any records to indicate your ward, Evelyn, has a burial lot as the family insists." I will help Evelyn find an alternative spot for her everlasting catnap.

6. Carla, a nursing home administrator, "I am expecting behavior issues from three of your wards…" These mentally ill men will have to make a choice between cable

TV and Marlboros. The new cigarette tax is at work.

Enough.

I get to *St. Mary's Hospital* to see the new *new guy*, and recall that Joseph another of my wards is a patient here too. I walk in confused circles because that's what I always do in huge institutional buildings.

I find Joseph first. He has been here a week. Among the 20 diagnoses listed on his chart, is HIV Positive. He is happy to see me. He tells me, "You're too fat."

It's part of my job to love this guy.

He recently inherited $100,000 from an uncle's estate. So far, I have purchased a $9,000 Scoot-About and a $10,000 prepaid burial plan.

It's now time for the nursing home to start biting into that $100,000 apple.

I wish he was well enough to take a trip, or do something memorably foolish, but he is too damn frail. He has siblings and cousins. But no one ever calls him.

I look at my gut and determine Joseph is right, I do need to lose weight.

Eventually, I find the *Intensive Care Unit* and look in on the new *new guy* from the hallway. His nurse is extremely busy and extremely beautiful. The new guy is not on a ventilator yet. He is pale, pale and pale.

The nasal gastric tube is jammed down his nose.

The oxygen mask fits snug on his face.

His hands are in restraints.

Monitors flip tiny beeps.

His eyes are open.

He doesn't see me.

His mouth is open too wide.

I speak softly into his ear, "Hello…"

No reaction.

Again, no family. No one available to sit with him through the dying process.

I read his chart and take notes in case the attorney needs documentation for a change in code status.

It's a busy unit.

I walk away wishing there were more staff to assist the patients.

I feel a little bit blue.

I fear I may never see the new *new guy* again. I wonder what his story is. I can't see him living too long.

It is after 5 p.m. I could visit one more person, so I go to the *Kankakee Assisted Living Center* on the southern outskirts of town.

I'm here to visit 'Peaches'.

One of my co-workers set Peaches *free* four years ago. Freedom was moving from a warehouse full of people with mental illness, packed four to a bedroom to her very own mini apartment. The kind manager of the units makes special weekly stops at Walmart so Peaches can have her soft orange candy, root beer and generic cigarettes. I am the only person who visits.

She may have a son in a penitentiary.

I don't know.

It's funny to me when she introduces me to friends in the hallway as her *state guardian*.

She is always thrilled to see me.

I always give her two dollars.

She always says, "I love you."

Bye.

I get in the *state car*.

Tomorrow, I have to recreate 'today' in case notes. If I find time between phone calls.

I feel blessed to have these people in my life.

I drive south.

Hope

When I go to the Dollar Store, I am mostly pleased. One can fill up a basketful of things to tidy up one's body, or clean the floor of one's kitchen. I have always believed linoleum reaches its zenith, after a generic *Mr. Clean* product, mushrooms into an infectious cleaning.

I buy sponges with scrubby surfaces on one side. I buy toilet cleaner. I buy a long-handled dustpan. I buy three cans, of chunky peanut butter. I buy body wash, for my body. There's always a line of other people buying $1 items. They're selling yesterday's newspaper. The cashier doesn't have the kind of job where one can fantasize. She has a merciless expression on her kisser.

Outside the Dollar Store, a young woman—I'd say she's 170 pounds wet or dry—is holding a sign, written on a piece of cardboard twelve inches by nine inches. The magic-marker indicates times are rough. She could use some of America's spare change.

She doesn't have a place to call a living quarter. I dig into my pocket and give her seventy-nine cents. She doesn't appear to be happy. I bet she doesn't get a lot of pennies. I note her brown hair, is greasy but still pretty. She's wearing bowling shoes, I think.

I walk across the parking lot.

Some kind thought swarms under my hat, all around my beanie.

I could do more.

I could do more than seventy-nine cents. I could offer her a shower. I could let her watch cable TV. She could borrow my terry cloth robe. I don't use it that much.

I walk over to her again. She's probably thinking, 'Oh Great, more pennies.'

I'm rethinking my invitation to shower. But the *better divine messenger* inside me speaks these words to her. "You know, if I was homeless, the one thing I would miss more than anything else, would be to take a shower. So, I'm telling you, that you can take a shower at my place. The bathroom door has a lock."

She says, "Ok."

She lifts her butt off the crate, pulls her coat together and says, "Let's go Joe."

"Follow me." I say, "What's your name?"

"Hope!"

I always liked the name Joe, so I didn't tell her my name.

She carries a brown backpack. It has stuff in it. It's bulging with stuff. I guess I'm curious about it, but it isn't a profound curiosity.

I think about what a houseless person, might find of value in my apartment. The only pawn-able item might be my CPAP machine—which isn't working at full throttle.

I do have a penny jar at home, and an account at the *Lafayette Credit Union,* with a balance of $139.40.

I will discreetly hide my bank statements when she showers.

She's probably thinking what color towel she will get to use. She probably has concerns about adequate water pressure. She doesn't relate any of her concerns to me.

She follows me down the stairs. She takes her backpack into the bathroom. I hear a flush. I hear water running. I surmise she is going to use my Chicago Bears full sized towel. I wonder if she dries between her toes. I don't. I watch an episode of *Father knows Best*.

She's now been in my bathroom for forty-seven minutes. I take showers that last as long as an *oldie* on the radio. Yesterday, I bathed to *Love Grows Where My Rosemary Goes* by Edison Lighthouse.

You never know what the future holds for writers of your biography.

Hope comes out of the bathroom with my towel on her head. My terry cloth robe is wrapped around her tummy.

"Got anything to eat Jack?" She asks.

"Wonder bread and generic peanut butter."

"Sounds good buddy," she replies.

She stands at the kitchen counter, next to a gallon bottle of bleach, and spreads peanut butter, on the crusty end of the loaf.

Then she wants milk.

I give her milk.

It seems to help with her peanut butter.

My bathroom is a mess. Dirty clothes. A wet washcloth, and that mysterious, brown backpack sits on the floor, next to some clearly used Q-Tips. She has used my toothbrush. I wash my hands and look forward to better things.

I walk into the front room. She has fallen asleep on my green couch. *Hogan's Heroes* is on TV. I take her clothes from the bathroom, and put them in the washing machine down the hall.

She doesn't snore bad. I lock myself in the bathroom. I unzip her crowded backpack. There's a David Bowie T-Shirt on top. Below are framed photographs. There's a little girl on a ladder feeding a giraffe. There's a smiling family in front of a Fireplace. Lots of pictures plus a Phillips screwdriver.

She stays and sleeps on my couch for two days. She eats a box full of HoHo's. She flicks my blinds and opens the window. The blue sky sifts in through the screen. She wears one of my Chicago White Sox T-shirts.

I tell her, "Keep it Hope. It looks good on you."

Actually, that shirt would look good on anybody. "You are so nice to me. May I call you *old chum*?" she asks.

"Yes, you can call me old chum."

She never opens up to me about her past.

My past is the stuff hanging on the walls. I have gone through a phase of my life when *Farrah Fawcett* was a consequential figure. Farrah's raggedy pictures have been through six different moves with me.

I have a ticket stub, on the Fridge from *The Tomorrow Show,* when Tom Snyder visited Chicago. He interviewed Wolfman Jack. I also have Van Gogh's print of *Starry Night*, held up with four industrial thumbtacks, hanging over my big, fat, television set.

She must have marveled at my things.

Anyone would.

Hope keeps her thoughts to herself. She has pretty good manners. She fixes Kraft Macaroni and Cheese for us, with bite sized hot dogs, that have done some marinating for a bit, in the cheese sauce. We watch a movie on the VCR. It's a *Don Knotts* movie about a fish. She has a good sounding giggle, when Don Knotts gets jittery. Before I go to bed. I give her a brand new, soft bristled toothbrush.

I lie in my bed. Why didn't she thank me for the shower, the macaroni and the toothbrush? I can't help but wonder where she is from, or who the people are in the photographs in her backpack.

I get up during the night to go pee-pee. I watch her sleep on the couch from a gentleman's distance. She has that snore. I go back to bed and think to myself *you know I don't mind a snorer*. I listen to a sports talk show, on AM radio. This guy on the radio knows everything. I wish I did.

When morning comes, Hope has gone with dawn's fog. She left a note, "Thanks old chum, you made me feel like I'm gonna be ok."

I feel an emptiness right above my belt buckle. I don't have a lot of friends, and when the possibility of a person, with whom I can share an idea with, goes away, I sadden up. I liked being an *old chum*.

Later in the day, I go walking.

The breeze pushes me into walking by that Dollar Store.

I don't see any Hope anywhere.

I go home.

New Year's Resolutions

I resolve to use the word "Frick" as purely a noun.

I resolve to quit confessing my transgressions to my dry cleaner.

I resolve to stop altering my 89-year-old mother's living will, just for laughs.

I resolve to get more exercise therefore I will stop using the motorized shopping cart, at Walmart to get home.

I resolve to stop taking topless selfie's.

I resolve to find something nice today about Berwyn.

I resolve to spend less time with my family, and more time watching Family Feud.

I resolve to learn something that I used to know how to do.

I resolve to break a 33 ⅓ record.

I resolve to make the unusual usual.

I resolve to participate in a kind gesture every six months.

I resolve to start buying *scratch off* tickets at a Lucky Gas Station.

I resolve to do less laundry, and use more deodorant.

I resolve to stop loitering at the laundromat.

I resolve to postpone happiness until it is convenient.

I resolve to make a new friend outside the Cook County Jail every week.

I resolve to be less judgmental regarding man buns.

Mom

She opened her eyes to electric light at The Loretto hospital. It was a frigid January day in 1935. An exhausted nurse placed a squirmy infant on the mother's chest. Everything was fresh, in the peering eyes of baby Geraldine.

She made eye contact with her red-haired mother.

It was at this moment, my mother Geraldine, obtained the abilities of crying, of grasping a finger, and of staring into the loving eyes of her mama. A switch had been turned on, and Geraldine began observing, creating and remembering stories.

It was a two-bedroom apartment, that now housed six persons. It was right above Geraldine's grandparents.

Geraldine's first entrance into the apartment, was to an unexpected party where she was passed around, from her oldest sister Jean, to Marge, to Fran, and then back to mama. The apartment was filled with smiles, and a pure joy.

Pure love behind toothy grins.

All the sisters had years of exceptional beauty. My mother's mother turned the flat into an embraceable home.

Geraldine's father, who went by the nickname Bus, walked up to the second-floor apartment, powdered with filthy clothes, layered in coal dust from his railroad jobs. He lived with the unpredictable expectations of five females. Three in Catholic school uniforms, each going in different directions.

There was fear in Bus's heart, that the sisters would eventually bring boyfriends—perspective husbands—up the stairs for a parental *look and see.*

There wasn't much in the way of fine furniture.

More like life within a black and white photograph.

Cameras clicked during good times.

Hard times were not going to be framed, or hung on the wall over the Davenport.

There was anger, and shouting, and perhaps madness, and sometimes, slammed doors. There was teasing by Bus, and there was baking by Mama.

There was a surprise one day, when Bus brought a baby alligator home, and housed it in the claw bathtub.

As a little girl, Geraldine's parents drove the family in an unreliable car with bald tires and a thirsty radiator to a cabin in Wisconsin. The apron of the cabin was a beautiful sand beach attached to the Wisconsin River.

To Bus, the cabin was not the thing.

The thing was standing in waist deep River water, and slapping the fast current with his fly rod line and tiny fly bait. Anticipation of a big Bass helplessly being reeled in to provide entertainment and story fodder, for the fellows when he got back home.

To Mama it was more work than usual.

The girls had debates on who looked the best in their swimsuits. Or, how to talk Papa into taking them uptown, with the possibility of meeting a new beau in Spring Green.

Once, Geraldine—at eight years old—was sent to a local Spring Green farm to buy fresh eggs. Frank Lloyd Wright was there. He patted Geraldine's brown hair, and asked the farmer, "How could you possibly take money from this little girl?"

Bus took the girls in a tiny wooden boat, on individual trips. He would tie hooks on the line with a unique knot. He tightened sinkers on the line with his teeth, and put the hook right through the minnow's eyeballs. It was hard to watch. The minnow would last three casts, before dying. But the bright scales on the minnow being reeled in, caught occasional sunshine, and irregular bites from river swimmers under the dark water. Geraldine would do her best to keep the tip of her line up, as instructed. But she would have easy distractions. The river's current created tiny whirlpools, that sparked imagination.

The river was so opposite of the Chicago where she lived. Everything was squashed into that apartment. There was nothing calm to stare at.

The river had all the space in the world.

It was exciting to get our feet wet. It was fun to see Mama and Papa get along, re-creating dreamy moments of their past.

Geraldine didn't know why her sisters couldn't wait to get back to the apartment. Geraldine would have stayed longer.

Everyone was cranky on the ride home.

Even crankier when a tire blew, and Bus cursed at everyone.

But mostly cursed under his breath.

Unfortunate Times

His world seemed to tighten like his 38-inch Levi's around his waist. Nothing good was on the horizon. Nothing consequential was swarming around inside his brain yet. Then, a stigma of anxiety clouded his thinking process. He had a premonition. No, it was a hunch. Something was going to go wrong.

He would have these gut level warnings every so often. The 3rd cup of coffee was nudging his apprehension. He wished he had ownership of any upcoming struggle that he might get a specific warning. But all he had was *something was going to go bad*. It was like an animal in the wild, received forewarning of an upcoming storm. The feral animal might find a hole in the tree and wait until it stopped raining cats and dogs.

He had wide open eyes. It was midnight when he left the bar. It was now 1 a.m. at the diner. He left a $10 bill for the bill, and tip. With every step toward the door, he could feel a half gallon of coffee, manipulate with the five old Milwaukee drafts he had drunk earlier. It was a familiar song and dance for his body functions to iron out.

Rain sprinkled at a steady drizzle. The car door handle wasn't locked. It was cold. Once he established his driving position, he flipped on the wipers. They smacked the drizzle away, with some degree of seriousness.

Home was only 15 minutes away, unless this hunch was going to turn messy. He wondered why his self was the one to be in possession of shit that might happen. He took one hand off the steering wheel and he removed his glasses. He wiped the lens clean with his flannel shirt. He put the glasses back on his nose while he turned from Main Street, to Arcadia Street. He glanced at the rearview mirror. A very big man was sitting in the backseat pointing a pistol at him. He pondered why God was giving him an insufficient heads up with a hunch this time. Life can be extremely cruel at unfortunate times.

"Where are we going?" Asked the man in the rearview mirror.

The driver pulled the car over to the curb on Arcadia. He shifted the transmission to the green *P* for park. He wasn't prepared for questions. He imagined the life remaining, on his personal parking meter, was less than 30 minutes. He began to draft up regrets. But the man in the backseat repeated his question.

"I was going to my place," said the driver.

"Good enough. Let's go," said the big man.

"Okay."

"What's your name?" asked the big man.

"Hank."

"Perfect. Put her in drive Hank. We'll watch some TV in your living room."

Hank did as he was asked. He never got a *full story*, when he got these hunches. Maybe he'd withstand. Maybe he'd have another imperfect evening of five beers and 3 cups of black coffee.

"Do you have anything to eat in your fridge Hank?" Asked the big man.

"Bacon and eggs. Stuff like that," answered Hank.

After Hank said that, he thought it was stupid. Nothing was stuff, like eggs and bacon. Hank pulled into a gravel driveway, and parked the car in front of a tiny house. The lawn's grass was probably 13 inches high. Hank figured the less he spoke the better chance he wouldn't piss off the big man.

The front and back car doors opened simultaneously. Hank climbed out and stood. The big man had crutches. He couldn't hold the gun at Hank.

Hank could have run.

Hank stood still like a frozen doe.

The big man was missing half of his left leg.

"Okay Hank. Let's go," said the big man. Hank fumbled with the keys, until he found the one with the green dot. He pushed open the front door. He held the door open. The big man stammered his husky body inside, and sat down on the couch.

As he promised earlier, the big man turned on the TV. Hank saw that the bandaged stump had spots of blood seeping through. There was a foul odor too. Hanks cat jumped on the couch, and placed itself on the big man's lap. The big man was amused by this. He laughed out loud. Hank was surprised the cat didn't shave his premonition.

"How about them bacon and eggs?" said the big man.

Hank took off his old junior-college windbreaker, and headed into the kitchen.

"What's your cats name, Hank?"

"Captain!"

When Hank delivered the earlier, earlier morning breakfast to his guest, the big man actually slid the gun over on the coffee table.

"Thanks Hank."

Hank settled in a comfy chair in the living room. He watched the big man eat and watch an episode of Charlie's Angels.

"Are you going to kill me?" asked Hank during a commercial.

"I might, and I might not," said the big guy.

"I'll trade you my car keys, for my life. I won't say nothing to nobody," pleaded Hank.

"I'll think about it," said the big guy. The show returned. The angels were wearing bikinis. The big man wiped his eyes often. He was probably tired, thought Hank. Being evil might be exhausting.

Hank saw a way out. He noted the big belly on the big man. It took him a good while just to sit up straight. Hank saw the gun was still on the coffee table, next to the greasy paper plate. Hank could run out to the front door, maybe grab the crutches, and throw them onto the lawn. He could get into his car and speed off. He could do this. He could do that.

Instead, Hank ambled passed the big man and slipped out the front door.

There was a policewoman on the stoop. She said she was there to deliver an urgent message. Hanks father had fallen in his kitchen. He was at Saint Joseph's emergency room. Hank was needed at hospital.

Hank told his story to the policewoman. He was ushered into the backseat of a squad car. Cherry lights of police cars hazily beamed through constant precipitation. Hank looked at his house. The big man squinted back at him, through the blinds. More cops appeared at the scene. Nobody shot nobody. Four uniformed cops carried the handcuffed big man toward the ambulance. The policewoman followed with the crutches.

A half hour later, Hank was sitting in room number 16 of the emergency room. He held his father's hand. Hanks father was in a cavernous sleep. Hank was afraid to sleep. He was afraid of unfortunate dreams this morning.

Christmas Card Letter

JANUARY

I joined a group for folks with uncontrolled neck hair beards. It was different. I was wearing a red coat after a kid told me that he blamed me for the worst Christmas ever. I told him he must be talking about my brother.

~ ~ ~ ~ ~

FEBRUARY

I invested all the money in my 401k into a Broadway musical production of Clutch Cargo and Paddlefoot. It was a scam. Fortunately, I only lost $27.53.

~ ~ ~ ~ ~

MARCH

I vacuumed some of the stale fries from my car for the first time in 43 months. I changed my sheets. I was mooned by kids on a yellow bus for the first time in 42 months.

~ ~ ~ ~ ~

APRIL

I helped my mom cheat on her taxes, for the seventh year in a row.

~ ~ ~ ~ ~

MAY

I was told by a bald elevator security guard that my behavior on the elevator was wrong. He gave me a brochure about an elevator etiquette class that cost 20 bucks. I took it. It was held in five different elevators throughout Chicagoland. I no longer press all of the buttons.

~ ~ ~ ~ ~

JUNE

I retired from almost 40 years at being a social worker to become a guy who is totally lost confused and somewhat happier. I found there is a strong correlation between viewing Netflix and gaining weight.

~ ~ ~ ~ ~

JULY

I was standing in line at the *everything is a buck* store. I noted that one could purchase a pregnancy test for a dollar. I don't know why, but I bought nine of them. I wondered if they might work on my cat.

~ ~ ~ ~ ~

AUGUST

I carried two Folgers coffee cans full of coins into my bank to be counted. The teller told me they don't have a coin counting machine anymore. So, I dropped a can on my favorite toe. It still hurts. I thought our president may be on a coin someday, but he's going should be *huge*. Perhaps we should name manhole covers for him.

~ ~ ~ ~ ~

SEPTEMBER

I realize that I didn't miss smoking as much as I thought I might. I miss throwing the butts out the car window at pedestrians.

~ ~ ~ ~ ~

OCTOBER

I was invited to join a group of guys who fantasized about football. I had to drop out because try as much as I could, I fantasized about other shit.

~ ~ ~ ~ ~

NOVEMBER

I sent a spit sample to Ancestry23.com. They determined that I was from a country called Berwyn, that my mom chews juicy fruit, that I was unhirable, and that everyone in my family tree had done time in Cook County.

~ ~ ~ ~ ~

DECEMBER

I write a stupid Christmas letter.

~ ~ ~ ~ ~

Bubbles

I crawl into bed beside Bubbles. She's already mashed to her capital CPAP machine. It pumps air into her face. It's kind of like I'm sleeping with Mrs. Hannibal Lecter. But I give the girl a break. She's got issues about the fate of reality TV celebrities or about the fate of her daughter's new racist prison guard not meeting her expectations. She has concerns about having received mail from AARP. How did they know how old she was?

Her diagnosis, like the sleep apnea, comes in a package deal with obesity, hypertension and diabetes type one or two—I don't recall—big bruises due to her Coumadin medication, and the rectal prolapse. Oh yeah, the heartbreak of psoriasis is planted on her right elbow and now she suffers from the depression. She claims the Prozac has killed her libido. Bubbles' cholesterol though is pretty good, pretty good.

The CPAP machine put the kibosh on her walrus tusk snores, which is a blessing. But the dog, Smoky—also obese, blind, and subject to epileptic spells has a significant snoring issue.

Here I lay, listening to the sounds of the night: a buzzing CPAP machine, a Lab/Shepherd snort, and drips from the kitchen faucet, and from the bathroom shower head—Ping Pang, Ping Ping. And every so often, a rollicking choo-choo train shack, shakes this 47-year-old trailer. I look up at the stain on the ceiling. It is a ringer for a fat pork chop. At least, at the very least, the trailer is almost paid for. Well…what is three, and half more years of monthly payments of $211.

It's chicken shit. And with Bubbles helping me with her government checks and with the prospect of 300 stimulus checks from

President Bush, life is as good as it's going to get. Sure, I get down about stuff. But Bubbles has made me think about her, instead of me.

I think she has that restless leg syndrome too. Her leg rattles the entire bed. Her Chicago Cubs T-shirt got the shilly-shallies like a boiling stew. I'm sure she'll get a pill for that leg thing too.

How does one get to the place where we are at? I never signed a contract of hope. I am a fat man living in a trailer for some happy and some unhappy days. I'm cohabitating. I'm still married, so I'm an adulterer. I never dreamed I'd become all of this.

I'd like to get unmarried or even better, become a widower but it ain't happening. The wife left me for a tortured keyboard playing ex priest. They live in a suburb of Cincinnati. He has a bad habit of chewing Redman tobacco and using a chalet as a spittoon. I'm hardly going to risk a long trip to Cinci to see what-is-what? I still receive her subscription of Architectural Digest.

One night about three weeks ago, Bubbles woke in the middle of the night having dreamt she'd won that $276 million lotto. The dream was so real she got up and wrote checks to her friends for $350 each! The checks still sit on the Emerson stereo speaker without stamps. We can't afford a book of forever stamps and she's going to annihilate her cute checking account into Armageddon.

She felt silly about it in the morning.

She said the first thing she did in her dream, was to purchase four new Michelin tires for my Datsun truck. If only dreams could come true.

I can't get to sleep. Staring at the pork chop only makes me hungry. I'm not a sheep counter. Maybe, I'll try to imagine I'm Dale Earnhardt's nodding dog in the rear window; Pretend I'm counting

Brickyard laps. I fall into a pitfall of cheaper trailer sleep. The pork chop is being paired down, with cutlery visions into bite-size pork snippets.

She is already up. She starts the new day with a too tight T-shirt that states, *My soul thirsts for God, for the living God, Psalm 40:12.*

I hear the floorboards. They elicit tiny shrill songs after each of her steps.

Am I thirsty for God this early?

It ain't even Sunday. Does one thirst for generic coffee, and menthol cigarettes? Yes, that is the mobile home of worship that grips my soul day after day maybe topped off with a caramel bear claw.

I piddle in the pokey with the door open. Over the stool is a crucifix; Jesus hanging with one arm. I keep thinking of putting Jesus back into his more comfortable tortured position, with some gorilla glue but something always comes up. We allow the good Lord to hang in extra anguish, pain and confusion as we brush our teeth. Nobody told Jesus about us. Bubbles has decided to display her collection of duck billed platypus figurines atop the toilet lid. One of them has a remarkable resemblance to Dr. Phil.

As I light the first cigarette of the perpetual life with my Dale Earnhardt zippo lighter, I see Bubbles allowing our doggy outside, to the great outdoors of our front porch. Smoky has developed a system of peeing between yellow two by fours. No steps for him. He wants back in.

He yearns for the life we are leading. He lies down next to my Zebco rod and reel, that lies proudly next to the entertainment center. A dried up nightcrawler is clutched to a rusty treble hook. Smoky's exercise routine is finished. He can resume snoring as Bubbles pours his generic dog food into a bowl that says Buck.

Buck was my former dog. He was put down to sleep due to a court order. He lost it at mom's nursing home. Buck bit the right breast of the assistant activity's director. I don't really know what happened.

Instead of the weather channel or CNN, Bubbles is still a stalwart VCR gal. She has us watching a movie called *Bachelor Party 2* as early as 8 a.m. She pours coffee into my cup that states *"Everything I like is either immoral, illegal or fattening."* An intoxicated elephant is in a dance mode, on the outside of the cup. I hope no one thinks I'm a Republican due to this elephant. Bubbles has her blue Cub hat on, the color matches her sapphire eyes. Even though I already know, I ask, "So what are your plans sweetheart?"

I hear, "I have an 11:10 appointment with Dr. Wallace regarding my psoriasis and I want to ask him questions about tattoo removal." Something like that. She adds, "Then I'm supposed to meet Kathy Ringelstetter, at the DQ for our weekly peanut butter Parfait." I love when she speaks French, "And I might go to the movies with Julie. I want to see *Bachelor Party 3*."

She sucks in her smoke. I don't know where it went. She eats careful portions of Lucky Charms. She looks around the room over her mug of sweet coffee and she parks her blue eyes on me and my face. It's one of those Kodak moments.

I took her in, after her *maybe husband* went to jail, for trying to buy excessive amounts of cold medicine and Charmin toilet paper from Sam's. No one had paid the lot rent. I saw her sitting on the porch of trailer number 37 smoking and crying and smoking in-between teardrops. She had a Comcast remote control in her breast pocket. She was locked out. Nowhere to go.

I seen her baggage right there that day. The suitcase had a tag that said *Bubbles*. So far, we've had two months of cohabitation. Her tearful, faraway eyes are what arrested my development. I opened the door to Trailer number 43 and I had a roommate just like that.

She could just kind of look at me. Her look made me want to stand up, open doors for her and possibly reach over the barbed wire fence, for a wildflower to give to her. I would put my hand in my pocket, and give her all my paper money. It was like I was in a trance.

Smoky cut a deadly fart.

I thought I should buy him a better brand of dog food. I am back to reality. Bubbles brushes her lips against my cheek, and nose. She waves goodbye through the not so squeaky anymore screen door thanks to WD-40. She leaves me under a spell.

I go to Citgo. They have a little area where guys like me can watch people pump gas into their gas tanks. The guy at the cash register gives me a senior discount on coffee but not on Long Johns or pastries. I listen to guys who go by nicknames. They bitch about their kids or wives. Bud is embarrassed because his wife shamed him into sitting on the stool all the time. Me, I am not complaining about my life with Bubbles.

The lights are on in the trailer as I pull up. There is a bucket of seashells on the porch. Usually that spot is where we keep the broom and mop. My gut tells me something is wrong. I have this internal fear that Bubbles will emancipate herself from our home, and float away.
There is Bubbles sitting at the table constructing a *Dear John* letter with a red sharpie. There's a man in the middle of the room holding some of her clothes on hangers over his back. His eyes are focused on a rerun of the Carol Burnett show. Bernadette Peters is singing a lively version of *"I don't know how to love him"* from Godspell, or Jesus Christ Superstar.

"Who is this?" I ask Bubbles. She continues to write. "What are you writing?" I ask.

"Honey, this is Corky Dubois. I met him at the Tivoli theater. Something happened between the two of us."

I look down. Corky politely excuses himself and walks around me.? "Sweetie, I don't want a letter from you, I want you to stay."

Smoky growls at Corky after Corky knocks over Smoky's food bowl. Tiny niblets of dog food scatter across the floor like stars might appear on a hazy narcotic linoleum sky. I imagine Smoky biting the unsocked ankle of Corky Dubois.

I'm hoping Corky will suffer with heart worms that exist in the hearts and minds of the canine populace but Smoky leaves confrontation up to me. Smoky chooses to release a fart, and dart into the bedroom probably to sleep under the bed. The bed that had had so many lost possibilities.

Bubbles doesn't offer to clean it up. Corky is carrying the CPAP machine with all the cords and tubes squirting out of a brown Piggly Wiggly grocery bag. I look at the kitchen table. I can see what Bubbles has written around her chubby fingers. She's moving on, up to a double wide trailer, satellite television, Pella windows, and a toboggan. The mood ring I had given her two weeks ago is changing colors. It indicates blue. I start feeling blue.

"It's not anything to do with you honey, I'm just accustomed to more from life than you can offer me," says Bubbles.

The blues. Everyone who ever recorded a couple of albums, has a song that ends with that word. Blues. *Reservation Blues, Dead Alley Cat Blues, Lost my Front Tooth Blues, Maraschino Cherry Blues,* and for me;

Girlfriend ditches me for the splendor of a double wide mobile home
Blues.

I sit across from her. She finally meets my gaze. Then, she looks away. I light a fresh cigarette and note I already have one lit in the Vegas ashtray.

Corky finally speaks, "Everything is on the porch, Bubbles. I'll get Leon's station wagon. We will get the hell out of here".

The TV is now showing a Dean Martin roast of Orson Welles. Don Rickles jokes about the girth of Orson. It's funny.

Bubbles tries to get out of the chair. She uses the shaky kitchen table as a support. The ashtray slips, but doesn't hit the floor. I watch her get off the vinyl chair, for maybe the last time. She struggles but she stands.

"You know Buttercup," she says to me, "There is a potato baking in the oven. Your microwave is on the fritz. And truth be told…sometimes, love is not enough."

"I guess not Bubbles," I answer.

"I guess not." She motions toward me and I back up.

Now I am a man who knows not when I'll be touched again. I used to subscribe to a promiscuous lifestyle, but I have had trouble finding a partner. I learned to substitute love with other stuff. You know. Malt liquor, filtered cigarettes, parking my ass at Citco and fishing for catfish with stink bait. But I am a man who presently feels like I'm a fiery piece of dog shit on a cement stoop who has been stomped on by a woman with elephant calves and Ked sneakers.

I look into her mesmerizing eyes. "Bubbles, I don't care if you and Corky are happy. I hope you both take a flying fuck at a rolling donut."

31

She stumbles out the screen door. I close the door behind her. I am hoping I have butter and sour cream for the baked potato. A rerun of *Three's Company* is just starting on TV.

2:37

A loud diesel truck zoomed by my window. It rattled the storm windows. It rattled my body and soul out of a deep sleep. My eyes open. I look straight up into the darkness of a ceiling. I do not know where I am. I can make out the form of a round light fixture and a vent of some kind above me.

2:37 is blinking in red light from a digital clock radio across the room. The blinking red light is what is giving this room any light at all.

There appears to be the form of another sleeper in the room.

I hear other strange noises from outside the room. Cars slipping by on the street. Motorcycles changing gears. Birds chirping. The birds probably aren't too happy about being woken by a noisy vehicle either.

I am disoriented but warm under the blankets that smell really fresh. I have a puffy pillow. I feel the fear of not knowing, but I feel the comfort too. If I listen really hard, I hear a faint television commercial from either outside the room, or from downstairs. Sounds like a TV psychic commercial I've heard before.

I hear channel surfing after the commercial.

I realize I have my jeans on. Fell asleep in my clothes. I dig deep into my jean pocket, and feel for the Red Bic lighter my boyfriend gave me for my birthday. A sense of relief when I find it. It's all I have left to remember him by. I hear steps. Someone's coming up the stairs. Keys jingle. The door creaks open a crack. The outline of a man comes to check on me. The light from the hallway enters the room briefly. I pretend to be asleep.

The door shuts. Keys rattle. Another door opens and closes. The man descends down the stairs. The other person in my room slept right through the whole lock, unlock, routine. There's a sense of security that the man didn't come close. No invasion. No touch. No rape.

I try to get back down into sleep.

I've been here before.

My new shoes are wet, cold and thoroughly miserable. The rain and cold is getting to me. I notice a Blockbuster video store across the street. It looks like a place where I can get some warmth.

Big posters tell me Blockbuster favorites are only $0.99 but only for a limited time. Computer beeps ping from the cash register. High-volume TVs blare above my head letting me know that heartthrob Freddie Prinze's new movie is now available. Freddie sits in a car with beautiful young actresses in the film clip.

A plain ugly young mother walks through a hallway with a beautiful baby in a stroller, and two little kids are crying because their mother won't let them have a movie. She threatens them with physical violence. "I swear, I'll beat your ass if you let go this stroller," she says to a teary-eyed toddler as she cruises slowly through the horror section of the video cassettes.

I stare at the baby in the stroller. The baby looks perfectly content as the siblings look miserable—because it's not a movie rental day for them. The mother picks out a movie: *The Texas Chainsaw Massacre 2001*. I have not seen that. Some of my friends have. They say it's pretty awesome.

As the stroller moves to the register, and exits, I walk up to the window to get one more look at the little baby.

I watch the mother put the kid in the car. I can't help but wish I had my own baby.

At one point, I wanted to have a mixed baby because I knew above all things, it would piss off my mother. My mom is ultra-prejudiced. She hates blacks. If I had a mixed baby, It'd pay my mom off for all the shit she put me through. She'd be so embarrassed. And it would be cool to have a baby. Somebody I could take care of. Somebody who would love me.

Since June, I don't worry about seeing my mom anymore. The state took custody over me. Since then, I've been from foster home, to group home, to where I am right now, getting warm in Blockbuster.

I've got a gym bag, that's on the concrete floor of my friend Stacy's garage. Inside are my belongings. I've got a copy of my favorite movies, *American beauty*, and *Bring It On*. They are so different. I've got my CD collection: I've got Nelly, and Snoop Dogg, and Dr. Dre, and Little Bow Wow, and Eve, and Pink, and TLC.

I let some kid at the group home use my *Discman*, and he dropped it. I beat the shit out of that kid, and then I ran away. I got things I stole from Victoria Secret. I got jeans I stole from Abercrombie and Bitch. I got lip gloss, shoplifted from Macy's. Come to think of it, I've stolen everything in this bag. Successfully!

There have been nights when I slept on the garage floor, next to the gym bag. Stacy snuck out once or twice and we smoked all her cigarettes. We talked around a candle all night long. Stacy's parents don't want her to hang with me. So, Stacy hangs with me to piss off her parents. Stacy brings sandwiches, and cookies, and Diet Coke. At least I always know where my stuff is.

Sometimes I think Stacy knows I'm out here and she chooses to watch movies and talk on the phone and do homework and play games on her Sony PlayStation or email her other friends. She lets her mom braid her hair instead of spending time with me.

This counselor, from Illinois Christian home is weird. I've already been asked every question a counselor, or social worker, or therapist, or psychologist, or shrink could ask me. Before he even starts on me, I start, "I hate men," I say. "I don't hate you I mean, but I don't trust men." I can tell that I threw him for a loop.

"Are you saying, you'd rather do this intake with one of our female staff?" asks the man.

"Did I say that?"

"No, but you said that you hate men." He runs his hand through his hair. He looks tired. He is sloppily dressed in a flannel shirt, and blue jeans. His eyes are tired. I can smell the aroma and hear the gurgle of Maxwell house in the Mr. Coffee. It's about 1:30 in the morning, when me and the squad car that brought me here, woke him up.

"Well, men have been abusing me, from the day I was born," I tell him. Knowing the *since I was born* part is stretching it. The bad memories of trying to escape being bait for mom's live ins won't quit playing over and over, in my mind like bad VH1 videos.

This man is trying his best. "I will guarantee you, Annie, that you will be safe here." He says, "We have a really good staff, and I think you'll like it here."

Then it comes back to how his tired body is really feeling like. "Why don't we just do the highlighted area of this intake form, and then I'll show you where you're going to sleep." He gets up, and pours a cup of black coffee into a Garfield mug, and sits back down. "We can finish the rest of the intake in the morning."

"Okay. What do you need to know so I can get some sleep?" I pull up my sleeves, forgetting that I had cut my forearm, with a razor blade a couple of days ago. And what's left, are bright red scab lines, up and down my forearm.

"What is that?" He asks.

I pull my sleeve up and show him, thinking the scars are pretty old now, and not really a big deal. He holds my forearm gently, puts on some glasses and stares at my arm. "Why did you do this to yourself?" He asks.

If he looks really good, he should be able to see, that I had cut my arm before. These are healed up scars. This is really no big deal. "I just wanna be able to feel something. I didn't cut myself deep enough to really hurt myself. I put some peroxide on, so the scabs don't get infected. I'd really like to finish this up so I can go to sleep."

"It looks like a suicide attempt to me," says the council. "I'm gonna have to call my boss, to see if we can keep you."

I know what this means.

It means that they're going to call a mental health worker, and they're going to see if I'm crazy. I will be sent to a hospital, where I will be in an emergency room for hours until I'm admitted to a psych unit. I've been through this whole shit before. "Please, please, please, just let me crash. I don't want to go through all this stuff. I really don't want to kill myself. If I really wanted to do it, I would have. I really know how, but I didn't. I just wanted to feel something. I like the way it looks when I'm bleeding. I am really OK." I realize I've said too much.

He tells me to lay on the couch, and he turns on the TV. Nickelodeon is playing an *I Love Lucy* marathon. I lay on the couch, and listen to him as he makes phone calls to his boss. I try as hard as I can to laugh at Lucy and Ethel stomping through damn grapes. But all I can do is cry. I want the counselor to leave me the fuck alone. And now they're going to mess with my head again.

I dig deep into my Pocket, and pull out a red Bic lighter. It sounds so stupid, but I kiss the lighter, because it reminds me of my boyfriend. I don't know where he is. I remember how good he felt. He looked like Mark Anthony. He was soft-spoken. He said he loved me. He said he wanted me to have his baby. We gave it a shot and if I am pregnant, he will find me and help me raise my baby.

My DCFS caseworker doesn't want me to see him because he's 22, and I'm 15. She doesn't understand that with all my life's experiences, I'm probably, really 32. She doesn't understand anything. She's a bitch.

I'm pretty mature for my age.

I lit a long cigarette butt, that I found in a sandy ashtray, outside the mall.

"Hey, Annie, how are you doing!" I realize that a guy I know from a former group home, is hollering out at me from a car filled with other guys.

"How are you guys doing?" I ask, trying to remember this guy's name.

"You don't remember me, do you?" He asks.

"Just the face, not the name. I knew when you lived at Concerta Hall." I tell him.

"Yeah, that's right. Do you want a ride?"

"That be great," I say climbing in. I grab a can of beer from what's left of the six pack on the floor and snag a joint that's floating around between the four guys in the car.

Alternative rock plays on the radio. Songs by Pete Yorn, and Cake, and the Lemonheads. The guys are really friendly, laughing and talking louder and then getting *touchy feely friendly*. There are hands on my boobs. I try to laugh it off. The driver pulls into a Bigfoot gas station, and the oldest looking one gets out to try and buy beer and cigarettes. I climb out after him, and feel hands on my ass as I struggle out the car.

I straighten out my top and then go into the gas station. I lock myself in the woman's john and pee. I wonder what I should do. I flush and fix my hair. I stare into the mirror at a condom dispensing machine on the back wall. Another machine will give you your weight, and your fortune for $.25.

I don't want to get back into the car. This pissing smelling john is a better place for me. There's a loud knock on the bathroom door, "Annie, are you coming?" I freeze, and stare at myself in the mirror. He pounds again. He yells, "Hurry up!"

I hear him calling me a slut, and telling me to fuck off.

When I'm pretty sure they've left, I drop a quarter in the weight fortune machine, and find out that I'm 125 pounds, and I'm going to have good luck, with money in the future.

I finally walk out of the bathroom. The Bigfoot employee is this pencil thin woman. She has the front door open. She has pretty, short, blonde hair. She's taking a break smoking. Her smoke goes out the front door.

"Do you think I could bum a smoke?" I ask her.

"Sure, honey," and she hands me a Marlboro. I reach into my pocket. I can't find my lighter. I must've left it in the car with those assholes. I feel like dying. This pretty lady with a Bigfoot shirt on lights my smoke.

"Are you alright honey?"

It was really nice to hear somebody call me honey, like they cared about me. This lady then gives me a Diet Coke and a slice of microwave pizza. She sure is nice.

This time, I am awakened by noises from downstairs. I think there's a cop downstairs. There is a cherry top, spinning blue and red lights, which form circular shadows in this room. I don't know why they always leave the squad car running.

I'm hoping I don't have to get out of this bed. I'm hoping the cop has brought someone else here and leaves me alone. I recall all of the "Do right, I've seen it all, you don't want to end up in the detention center, or even worse, found dead somewhere, better turn your life around," talks that have been delivered to me, by policemen and policewomen, in all shapes and colors, right before they leave you in another foreign place.

I hear the front door close and the sound of a squad car driving off. The round color lights extinguish. I am pretty convinced that a new kid was just delivered by a man in blue. The room again becomes pitch black except for the clock radio blinking 2:37 like it did the last time I was here. I know exactly what the kid downstairs is going through:

Reviews of house rules.

Questions about everything you could ever imagine.

And then they come up with a toothbrush, and soap, and sheets, and maybe a raggedy towel,

and set you up to sleep in a room with complete strangers.

Everybody should experience this just once.

The door to my room opens. I pretend to be asleep. New girl makes her bed. She changes into some on-loan sweats. Looks like she is comfortable with the routine. She walks over to a window, lifts the blinds and pulls the window up. She goes to her bag grabs something and climbs

out the window. I get up and look out there. She's sitting on the roof having a smoke. She's on the flat roof over the porch. I look at her. She looks at me and smiles. "Can I bum one of those?" I ask as I climb out.

"Sure, but you gotta return the favor when you have some," says the girl.

"Absofuckinlutely," I say, and she starts laughing.

We talk. She's a ward of the state. Her dad's in jail. Her mother's in rehab. She has a sister in a different foster home. I tell her my story. Both of us agree that the system sucks, that we wish our boyfriends were rescuing us, or holding us and that we both want to see the new Snoop Dogg video again.

It's really cool.

I can really feel the night air.

I can see the moon, and the stars above me.

I do not feel so alone tonight. I laugh for the first time in a while. I feel alive. We crawl back into the room after about an hour. We go to sleep.

800 Apple Street

I'm not in the business of waking up housemates.

I'm not even employed. In fact, I feel like a doofus knocking on his door.

But I do.

Howard's response is no response. It's a hush, harsher than Duran Duran playing on MTV downstairs. An extended coffee break of quiet. I know in the seconds I stand there, my housemate and friend may have pulled the plug on his unpleasant, for the most part, raggedy dance with his moving parts. He told me he'd do it someday. I'd nod and listen. But you know, there never seems a good time for your friend to die.

Before I allow my *in the hallway mind* to stray anymore, I open the door.

I holler his name.

I look at the top bunk.

There is no bottom bunk.

Howard is one very dead English major, *Illinois State University* student. His face is a low blue hue. Lips an ugly purple. I feel his face. Cold hard silly putty.

He could've mustered a, "See ya later, Gary." This was a fuck you fare thee well.

There's no blood. There aren't any guns, or knives, or razor blades, or ropes.

There are empty Osco pill bottles. He probably took a prescribed 'trip' that would lead to a furlough of infinity.

I forget myself.

I bawl.

John, another housemate, runs up the stairs and watches me linger next to Howard's end. He figures out the thing to do. The thing to do is to push and pull me back to the hallway. I'm a sad Sociology major.

Roger, another housemate runs up the stairs as John shuts the door. "You don't want to go in there," John tells Roger. And Roger doesn't.

I have a sniveling station outside the door. Jeb, the house dog, comes up the steps to see if he can help. I kneel and take in the gentle touch of the dog. It's a moment when you know who a real friend is. We just stand there. Four paws and two feet.

Someone must have called the cops. The ambulance guys run up the stairs at an urgent pace. One of them opens the door, climbs on Howard's chest and pounds futile thrusts of energy on his torso. I can't help but think the ambulance thumper is a fucking idiot. Dead is stapled and stamped all over Howard's form.

A death mist escapes from the open bedroom door. It wreaks senseless smog throughout 800 Apple Street in Normal, Illinois.

The ambulance boys transfer his starched body to a gurney. They put a blanket over everything, even his face. No part of me thinks of saying bye bye. It's an awkward march down the stairs and out of the front door.

They take my friend away.

I never see him again.

Minutes after he offed his self, our house, 800 Apple Street, once a party house on the apron of the ISU campus becomes numb. Thoughts and questions climb into my head:

'Who will rent that room after this?'

'Why will anyone climb these stairs except to take a shit in the john?'

43

'Who'd party here?'

'Now?'

It's going to be a different 800 Apple Street; A dark house of a different color.

We expect the police to do something.

They don't.

All the cops do is stand on our front porch and watch the gurney do the *dead man's coast* into the back door of the ambulance. They stand in some formal silence beside John and I. Nobody asks, "Who is Howard?"

Howard leaves the house in an exorbitant ride. Everyone is polite. The police get in their squad car, turn off the electric cherry top and disappear on Route 51 going north.

Tears of what my friend has done stay tucked into my tear ducts. I am going to have to get my shit together. I have this hollow hole in my consciousness. I thirst for a vice to be a friend.

Cigarettes and peanut butter work for some reason.

I want to tell Howard things.

But the thoughts no longer have a target. They fan themselves out with cold drafts through the rusty screens.

Death is an absence for me. The resignation of Howard's spirit is a kick in the nuts. This event erodes my earth.

Beliefs? Beliefs of my failure as a friend.

He tick-tocked away.

Deeds? What deeds would have him kicking for a few more hours, weeks or semesters?

I never expected him to become a Social Security recipient someday. I expected something. I assumed he'd graduate with a worthless degree in English. He could move to Chicago after college and kill himself there.

He wasn't a writer, but he could teach with his degree. I picture him sitting at a desk behind a chalkboard. He'd interrupt a discussion of Ivanhoe with his stately view of life to a crowd of sixteen-year-olds. He'd tell them, "Life sucks the Grand Wazoo." His marriage to depression brought out the nicotine from his Camels.

So, life doesn't always go on.

Sometimes it just drips shit on you.

Sometimes it expires with your Reader's Digest subscription.

We'd share a booth at a diner within rambling distance from campus. It became a custom for him to supply Camels, and my task was to pull crinkled green bills out of my Levi pocket and pay for our cups of mud. We'd talk for hours about stupid crap under a cloud of our own smokes.

It was like recreating under a 1962 Chevy tailpipe. A waitress kept the java streaming into our mugs. We weren't stimulating the waitress with our attempts at hand me down intellectual banter. We had coffee jitters, a poor man's Parkinson's disease.

We were invigorated with the fact that we may have actually become friends or as Howard said, "Almost friends." Our discussions might take off on Professor Bishop's preposterous propensity for saying "Um" too much. One time, we counted 31 "ums" in a one-hour lecture. We discussed ISU's unattainable female students and our mutual lack of a girlfriend due to little class, less cash. We littered our talks with profound quotes from our favorite album, *Nighthawks at the Diner*.

We lasted till closing time. Hints of the end of poor Berniece's shift were watching her stack chairs on tabletops. And Bonnie swept under booths with the passion of a sloth. She told us it was time to almost leave.

What we had was a steady pleasant enough flow of shitty verbiage.

But sometimes, Howard's ominous window of darkness cranked open for him to crawl out his prediction that one day, "I will commit suicide."

No one could pull the shades down on that window. It was always available to him.

A Turtle's Story

I have never been so scared in my life. Standing, sitting, or whatever it is us turtles do to deal with panic; that is what I am doing on this yellow strip in the middle of Route 67. If I had eyelashes, I'd shut them. If I had high blood pressure, I'd raise it.

I was just being a damn turtle.

What do we do with our days?

Well, we eat disgusting crap, we bathe in the sun on logs, and we have this bad habit of trying to cross highways. But now, I see huge rubber circles shimmy by my face at high speeds. I look down the road and *Syd the Snapper* has made it and I'm thinking.

I'm thinking I should turn back as I have made it halfway.

Even if the other side of the road is a blessed Garden of Eden.

Maybe the other side is not a utopia like Syd says. Maybe it is no good.

So, I am idle.

One wonders what a turtle, such as I, might ponder? I can't help but wonder how a single human shoe got to the side of the road? Were humans kissing and allowed their toes to stretch out the window in bliss and lose the sensation of a rubber boot? Plippety-plop. Maybe the boot was left to mark a spot on the highway – a spot to return to someday. Maybe it was cleverly tossed to become home to a big old muskrat.

A gigantic wheeled vehicle—I counted 15 rubber circles, maybe more—is stumbling crossly up the road. I see my friend Tony bouncing from wheel to wheel like a hockey puck. By the time the whoosh is over, Tony is on his back next to me. Whenever a vehicle comes by, Tony spins like a fallen ice-cube in the middle of the road.

"Hi Ralph," he says.

"Hi Tony," I answer. I know better than to ask how he is, us turtles get kind of weird when we are on our backs.

"You know Ralph, I woke up this morning thinking minnow. All I could think of was yummy minnow. So, I thought of crossing the road. I don't know why a chicken crossed the road but anyway, here I am."

There we is. We is together on the yellow stripe. Whooshes of human controlled vehicles zip by and poor Tony spins like an upside-down Eddy. I can hear him cry out as he spins, "Oh fook, Oh sheet!" As he spins down, he is too misconstrued to utter anything for a minute and then he is back in the ballet on Route 67.

I just cram in my shell and wait. My mama didn't tell me there'd be days like these. In fact, she just laid my egg and left me to fend for myself. There was no book of instructions for turtles. It was just an existence. Life was not sweet until I discovered live bait.

It may look like a pristine life to sit on a log and bake in the sun, but we are lost in our own reptilian thoughts. If only there was a good juicy novel and a fresh tidbit served to me on my log by a garcon turtle in a bowtie. I guess I can only speak for myself, but I've had to deliberate turtle issues like:

Fear of man.

Fear of a 75-pound catfish

Fear of that icy and cold shit that comes around and lasts forever

Fear of hooks.

Fear of bigger turtles knocking me off my log and the ultimate fear...

Spinning on your back waiting for a big rubber circle to squish you into crow food.

Life is not so great as a turtle. We can't even turn our mouths into a smile. Sure, we think of sex, but no one I know has ever seen their Johnson. Everyone in the swamp has had their way with *Wand the painted turtle*, but now we are afraid.

Afraid of sexually transmitted turtle disease with the rumored consequence of going blind, growing hair on out claws or being totally stuck inside our shells for 8 hours or more. I have enough trouble, thank you Wanda.

No one told me what a turtle's life expectancy is, so maybe I've surpassed it. Maybe I should just take my chances. I put my claw out. Tony screams, "What the fook are you doing Ralph?"

"I don't know," and I scramble back into my shell.

And then, my world turns upside down. In seconds, I am raised in the air by a human gripper, followed by Tony…seconds later. I am tossed into a new world of a pink bucket.

I recall not knowing the correct strategy. Is it to pretend I'm dead within the shell, or fight like a mean critter with wild swipes of claw and superlative yipping bites at the human gripper device?

I compromise and put my head and claws within and slap my tail about in an effort to free myself from the situation. Alas, I feel a failure sharing a pink bucket with Tony. I really don't like being squashed in a pink bucket with other turtles. It's not a big improvement. I wish it was a different colored bucket. I wish for a bigger home.

"Oh fook," says Tony.

"Oh fook, what?" I answer.

"Oh fook, you know this human is gonna turn us into soup or salad or soufflé' or something," says Tony.

"Oh fook, you don't know that. Maybe this human likes to do humanitarian things or turletarian things."

"Oh fook Ralph, we ain't never gonna chew on fresh minnow guts again, we ain't never gonna have turtle intercourse again."

"Oh fook," says Ralph, "We ain't dead. Keep a good fooking thought."

And we ride in that bucket down the road, imagining fooking bad scenarios with new turtles being picked up and plopped on top of us. And the truth is that they're heavy, even if they are my brothers.

Within the bucket, mucky liquids splash a warm bath of turtle urine on me and Tony; him with his fooking spirits of doom. I climb around 4 terrapins on the back of 3 red glider mouth turtles. My goal is to see what the human and his grippers are up to.

Is this my last day on this planet? And what's so great about humans anyway? Sure they invented buckets and yellow lines, but what's so phenomenal about these inventions? I look up at the human who has picked me up. He's mammoth. His shell or belly is only half a worm away from bumping the circle that steers this contraption. He only needs one gripper to navigate.

He looks over at me. I match his stare, but he quickly looks away. I can hear some noise from the car doors bellowing, "You light up my life." That's probably a bad sign for me as I like dark, dank places most of the time. He talks into a tiny box. I think about jumping out but I'd only land on carefully manipulated human garbage.

There's a big gulp cup, a wrapper from Quiznos subs, lots of red and blue cans, and lots of butts. The floor doesn't look like a good place to be. It looks like a place to put dead stuff. I wonder why a human moves dead stuff around with him.

50

The moving contraption we is in, slides into a big lot. Poufs of stone dust litter the immediate air and sky about us. The bucket slips over and all of us turtles are slipping and sliding in the dearth, the dearth of his contraption floor. I have had enough. I am always a guy who has had some semblance of control until this day of human terror.

The human picks us up one by one and puts us not so gently back into the bucket. I think we've all given up. We've never been exposed to prison escape movies with the exception of a teeny, green turtle who spent a year in a bowl on a coffee table, beside human feet resting upward like little statues, eating brown pellets and watching HBO. He was tiny and squeaky and couldn't raise our community in a bucket spirits to believe we could do anything. He spoke of human Steve McQueen of *Papillion* fame, and Linda Blair of *Woman in Chains IV* fame.

Anyway, the bucket had become home for us all once again and a turtle's anxiety made its best efforts to fill it up with turtle urine again.

I peek and note everyone except me, and teeny green guy are scrunched up in their shells, scared out of their wits and waiting for the end of the world. Meanwhile, the human walks and the bucket sways and he picks one of us out and tosses him off a long pier into a green pond. I see *little greeny* go in with a small splash as he reminisces about being Steve McQueen on a motorcycle in *The Great Escape*. I hear Tony spell out F.O.O. and K as he flies in the air and his rotten day turns out OK as he lands in a lovely mess of mosquito larvae. I too am in the air for seconds of fear before landing next to Tony. "Hey Ralph, this ain't so bad." He says.

"Tony, we got enough mosquito larvae to eat for the rest of our lives." I answer. Maybe this is gonna be okay.

After Eric

I can't really think since the accident. I can't fathom how I will be able to focus again since my little boy had an epileptic seizure in the bathtub and drowned on a warm February Sunday morning in 1998.

I can only exist in this rocking chair.

Good people drop warm dinners off at my house a week after my little boy died. I know their love and good intentions are baked into these tuna casseroles. The important issue to be worked out is, *how will they get that casserole dish back?*

I listen but I do not hear as my wife develops a plan to get the dish back to the friend, clean as a whistle.

Very soon.

I know these cheerful faces didn't know my son. They know of him, and his disabilities. But they always made a line in the sand. Enough space to keep a distance from his drool.

So anyhow, anyway…weeks pass.

The wife cries herself to sleep around me.

Around friends and family, she finds strength to clean launder and reheat leftovers. She is a profound weeper. Living in the house where he died every square inch is filled with memories of laughs cries bellows and frustrations.

I hear the knock on the door.

And I remain stationary in a rocking chair.

I hear someone wanting to recover their casserole dish.

Out the window healthy kids in a mini-van stare at the house where a kid drowned in the bathtub.

I feel as if I live in a ghost house in New Orleans.

Something mysterious and creepy.

Mail arrives with cards from faraway folks with checks for $10. People send poems about losing their favorite people. I find myself reading the lyrics of Stairway to Heaven:

And as we wind on down the road

Our shadows taller than our soul

There walks a lady we all know

Who shines white light and wants to show

How everything still turns to gold

Priests do this kind of thing all the time. Homilies welcoming souls into eternity. Since our priest never met Eric, I provide words to him so some of the little boy's personality is squeezed into the mass.

I consider a return to work. My daughter returns to school and has daydreams of her brother freezing under the ground of the cemetery in Edgar County.

Whatcha say to that?

I say nothing and hug my only living child.

Later I tell her, "I love you so much."

I do not know how the wife could have written *lesson plans* for substitute teachers the night of his death. But she did. I realize my own limitations. I can't get out of the chair because there isn't anything to get up for anymore. I know I'll be no good at my *social work job* for a long time. I find a 30-minute surprise vacation from grief in Seinfeld reruns.

Eric's short bus came by one morning after the death and beeped just like it beeped when it was pick-up time for *Sunnyside School.* The beep reminds me Eric is gone. I am a mess of tears and pain. My wife is even worse. My daughter splits time with both of us trying to help me try to cry less.

The bus driver delivers Eric's book bag to the weepy house.

I shower.

The pulsation feels good.

I look down at Eric's death spot at my feet.

How can I possibly do this every day?

Every time I close my eyes, I see my son under water.

I keep the door to his room closed. I don't want to change the sheets. I don't want to wash his clothes. I have this awful fear I will forget how he smelled. I want his smell in my shirt pocket so I can have him close to my heart. He has been bandaged by disabilities all kinds of interesting pain.

It wasn't minutes after he was dead that I realized how my life changed. I don't have shifts of the 24/7 parent of a disabled kid anymore. I don't have appointments with speech therapists or occupational therapists or academic individual program plans, with special educators.

I can disappear at a coffee shop and not meet with some professional who wasn't gonna do much for Eric anyway. Sure I still have two jobs, a house, debts, a wife, a daughter and a not-so-well-trained dog. Now I can watch the Bears without interruptions. I still have tears in my eyes.

I wish we could sit on the couch, and reread *Goodnight Moon* for the one-thousandth time and follow that mouse from page to page.

I sit at the Daily Grind coffee shop and write pages and pages of memories with the help of caffeine.

Tears fall on pages.

I wonder how long my heart will feel like it's grinding in neutral. I feel like I now belong to the most unblessed club there could ever be *parents who have lost a kid.*

There is news of some child's life ending in awful ways almost every day in the *Chicago Sun Times*. I write letters to people I don't know offering prayers to new club members. I can't find words. I can't find anything. I join organized grief groups. I can't deal with a woman who struggles with her mom's death.

She had the chance to say, "Goodbye!"

I had to pull a lifeless body out of bathtub water and run to the hospital wondering, *'Will he be resuscitated?'* Or *'Might he be even more severely retarded?*

I can't keep telling this story. I feel like a failure every time I tell it. I take my wife to a more specialized *Compassionate Friends* support group. I help her as she gets ill on the way home after hearing of the *torture of life without certain kids* for 90 minutes.

I know time doesn't really heal. My folks lost my sister 25 years ago. My mom tears up every time she hears Diane's name.

It was pretty awful to lose a sibling.

A best friend to suicide.

A dad too young to die of a heart attack.

But when you lose a six-year-old boy like Eric, I have lost my zeal. I feel horrible all of the time. I see possibilities of his sparkle in others and I cry.

I cry when I drive.

When I sit at my desk.

I cry when I take a walk and if you're like me you find a place inside your soul, and you hide.

I know already that the worst thing that could happen, happened. I discovered a long time ago that I wasn't one to holler or scream. I have a hard time getting angry.

I get mad at God.

I avoid God.

I wonder why He twisted my life to shreds.

I could get mad at people who tell me, "Eric is in a better place." Hawaii is a better place than Monticello, IL.

I could get mad at people who know Eric died but never mention it. I can't imagine how it can be that hard to say, "I'm sorry about your son, man." Well, it must be hard.

After a couple weeks people expect me to begin bouncing back and being *who I used to be*. My gut tells me most are burnt out from talking about it. I feel like getting a tattoo on my hand, so I never forget him. I am mired so deep in my personal malaise that I can only help my wife and daughter so much.

A day is cool 'til I find out my compact disc carousel does not work, because Eric must have jammed a tiny pair of scissors into the machine.

Nothing seems to matter.

I find out later from my daughter's confession that she stuck the scissors in there.

She is always forgiven.

I want nothing to do with holidays. Holidays throw around prospects of joy and tradition that I now hate. I go through the motions for my twelve-year-old. I wish she would pick the lifeless *Charlie Brown Xmas* tree. I realize how deep my love is for my living child. I tell her maybe twice a day that I love her. I get her out of *school band* over her mom's objections and feel good about that.

I think I might be better off dead.

I've discussed this with my wife and… she too, wants to die, to be with Eric, but we don't die, because of our living kid.

Casseroles stop coming. The gifted plants wilt due to *no focus* on reading the tiny plastic instruction card.

February turns to March and then April. I find reasons to get out of the house. Entering 805 Lincoln Drive is like a morgue of pain. My hand doesn't want to turn that doorknob.

I picture myself with a hole in my chest.

My chest beats anxiety.

I wonder if I will ever be the same man I used to be.

The dog circles the rug six times before lying down.

She looks at me with moist eyes as if to say, "I'm dealing with this too."

All That is Left of the Moon

She looks up. Her mouth shares a clothespin with a toothpick. She struggles against the wind, to hang a tiny *Detroit Tigers* jersey up in the summer breeze. The basket is full of multicolored, multi sized outfits. The wind and hues ultimately combine, to create an abstract backyard visual production.

Little tots run in circles, and celebrate sunshine, or react to scraped knees with resounding exaggerated tears.

An old dog looks up to the sky in frustration,

as if he sought a quiet corner where he could sleep,

without a diapered kid

being so curious about his tail.

The women tires of her life. She owns pain in varicose veins. Pain, in knowing her trucker husband is away. Probably having a coffee, and piece of chocolate cream pie, with a waitress at the *Dixie Truck Stop* in Tuscola, Illinois right now.

She won't get any relief from the kids, until they fall asleep on their superhero pillows. He really is good with the kids, when he is home. But he is always drowsy. He seems to want to be alone so much.

One never knows which mailman, or mail lady will eventually stuff the box with clutter. They'll be wearing those *government blue shorts*. A brief, "Hello" with any adult, is preferable to hundreds of kiddy chats, about who got hit, or,

"When will Daddy be coming home?"

"I'm hungry."

"I don't want to take a nap."

Anyways, everyone sits stationed in high-chairs, or on telephone books on top of chairs, in anticipation of a new day's lunch:

Plastic boxed bologna.

Plastic wrapped Kraft cheese slices.

Juicy Juice in plastic sippy cups.

And, a couple of very orange carrots, appear on the still syrupy, kitchen table.

The dog knows, this is his chance to *shine under the table*. The dog prevents sweeping projects, afterwards. The old mutt leaves his station, to *front door bark*. Which creates a whirl of curiosity for everyone. The woman runs to open the door, and retrieve the mail. She hollers a hollow, "Thanks," to a pretty postal carrier. She scoots back to the responsibility in the kitchen. She sorts through the mail.

The phone rings, it is the husband. He won't be home till really, really late. He is sorry.

She feels like throwing in the towel. She settles for wiping off three little chins, with a dish rag. The VCR and Scooby-Doo tape rescue her, for the moment. The kids all agree that the cartoon is the absolute bestest thing in the world. Even though it has been the bestest thing, twenty-seven days in a row.

She pages through a *Victoria Secret* catalog.

It makes her want to eat ice cream.

~ ~ ~ ~ ~

He pulls his semi over to a car wash. It is a deep side pocket part of the night. He finds a can of WD40. He steps out, and sprays oil on his clothes. He thinks the *hardware scent* will eliminate smells of the waitress he has just been with.

He closes his eyes,

and almost feels,

the cat-like caress of the waitress.

He boils over, with a tough bliss for the waitress. It's not anybody's fault. He can't stay loyal. Even the Good Lord, couldn't resist this cheese omelet server's goddess aura.

Shit.

Every time he smells bacon,

she appears in his notions.

The waitress, fries and curls around his brain.

The waitress expresses that she was unhappily married. He's not sure how one decides on happy. But three little pumpkins are going to roll into his bedroom next morning and joyfully celebrate his fatherhood. His wife is going to want something, he does not want to give up...sleep.

Jeez.

He hopes she doesn't want to pack everyone up for church, and a pancake Sunday breakfast. Watching his youngsters, play with different IHOP shades of syrup, is a world he didn't seek. Sometimes he gets home, and the wife disappears for hours. And he is, all of a sudden, host to Daddy responsibility.

His semi tries not to wake the neighbors. It still disturbs some canine spirits, who yelp at him, and what is left of the moon. He enters the house. She is breathing and slumbering on the couch. The carpet is littered with Lego's, and Barbie knockoffs.

He enters the bathroom, and enjoys a damp *Ladies Home Journal,* while he finishes his business. He finds a cold bowl of *Kraft Macaroni and Cheese* in the fridge. He negotiates his gastral yens, with the color orange.

The twenty-seven-inch TV sends flares and tepid firecrackers through the indoors of this fabricated home. Flicks of light tell the world that someone sent a check to the power company. He checks his pockets, and finds the waitresses red panties. He stuffs them back and walks outside, through the sliding glass doors into the cool, confused night. He throws the panties over a six-foot wooden fence. He lights a smoke from a hard pack, and tries to feel like smoking is why he came outside.

Inside, the wife is still asleep on the couch. He still smells of WD40. The kids will be up in two hours. He strips and tunnels into the unmade king-sized bed. He finds solace in sheets, and the smell of his wife.

The bed eventually calls to the wife. She curls into his unconscious un-aroused state. His cold feet don't bother her. She doesn't wake him. His body warmth reminds her of her childhood Collie, Ginger, whom she slept with growing up. She assumes the worst from her husband. He sleeps with jerky movements, like he is bathing in troubles.

She snaps her jeans, and pulls on a T-shirt, with Monarchs flying around a Sunflower. She stares at the doorknob; it offers opportunity. She sits on the corner of the bed, and peeks at the kid's doorways.

She ties her Nike's.

Sits at the kitchen table.

Scribbles a note to her husband,

Gone shopping.

She leaves a question mark, as to when she will return. She leaves her cell phone at home. She walks to the driveway and starts the minivan. She'd like to drive, and drive, and end up with her tires stuck in the sand of a glorious beach. She settles for a journey through a field of soy. There is no destination. Just the hope of letting her lungs breathe in a deep *Not*

Home breath. She had begun a sometimes routine of driving into Champaign. She parks downtown. She waits for a bus. She smokes on a bus bench. She watches others' lives flutter around her.

She loans matches to a couple, who have no light. The man lights a match and holds it lit, for what seems like a lifetime. He speaks about the previous night of drinking Tequila. The match looks as if it will burn his fingers. He lights the women's cigarette, then his own. No burns. He shakes the match cold and holds on to it. He continues to yap. She imagines what it is like to have a *life*, blown out with a whiff. Her life rattles in tiny winds. The bus blows into the bus stop the way her dog charges into his Alpo.

On the bus, she closes her eyes. The driver has *The Everly Brothers* swooning over a gal, on the transistor radio, taped to the dash. A man with a wonderful cologne, makes her think of Dad, on church Sundays. A woman talks about how to prepare pigs feet. Bumps on Main Street rattle the whole bus.

She opens an eye.

She is eye level with people's crotches.

Some folk smell like cattle.

Some are anxious to depart, so they can enter homes, that bring satisfaction. Some sluggishly remove themselves off the bus to earn paychecks on tips. It is 9 a.m. She has already ridden the entire loop. The driver shares eye contact with her. He must wonder what she is about. She sees the word *Teddy* tattooed on her inner ankle.

~ ~ ~ ~ ~

Bacon splashes grease on his forearms.

He yelps, "Shit!"

"That's a bad word!" says the oldest kid.

"Sorry!"

The kids pick *Lucky Charms* stale treats, out of the cereal bowl with enthusiasm. A kind of marshmallow and pork breakfast. He still smells of WD40.

The fried bacon makes him smile, with very recent nookie memories. A pile of crisp slices build on a paper plate. Breakfast with Daddy is fun 'cause the sippy cups are full of *Grape Kool-Aid*. The kitchen cable TV plays NASCAR wrecks. He tunes out the kids to gain new Earnhardt knowledge from the show.

The phone rings. He lets the machine answer. It's his folks. They want to know if he and the kids are coming to the church potluck. He rarely talks to her folks and she never talks to his.

After the feast of grease and whatever marshmallows are made of, Daddy fills the tub with water, toys and Mr. Bubbles. It is a splash fest, until he wraps them in *Dr. Seuss* towels. He tries to find diapers, undies and clothes that will not match. The kids get loose, he smiles. He flies about the house trying to scoop up their cherub bodies. He has no clue when the wife will return. He doesn't care too awful much, about that.

He looks at his forearm, and the word *Teddy* sealed in a green tattoo, with a tiny frog. He…well, actually, he and her, lost their Teddy, a few years ago in a car crash. He couldn't keep a picture of Teddy in the bedroom, because it makes her cry.

He lost everything happy.

He is just starting to feel raindrops of life again,

right now, from the bacon.

The kids fight over control of the remote. He should make them all watch the NASCAR channel as punishment. He settles on a live action

64

Scooby-Doo tape. He doesn't like Blue's Clues anyway, and Scooby-Doo farts are funny.

~ ~ ~ ~ ~

She makes her final round. She likes the bus ride, because it is the only time someone does something for her. The glass doors of Wal-Mart welcome her to a clean warehouse of new stuff that she doesn't have much of. She circles the place three times without putting anything in the cart. She told her kids she will never take them down the cereal aisle again, until they are eighteen.

She sees other kids having serious cereal conversations, with their mothers. Mom's surrender to Count Chocula. She finally reloads on Lucky Charms, and Nestle Nesquik.

~ ~ ~ ~ ~

One thing that was fun, was the minutes before bedtime. All five or six would sit on the couch, and read a story. From outside the picture window, one might see them as models for a *Norman Rockwell Saturday Evening Post* cover. They turned the chewed-up pages of *Goodnight Moon*. They followed the teeny mouse, from paged adventure to adventure. The old lady told them to, "Hush." Then Daddy carried two toddlers, like footballs, into beds that welcomed them, with quilts of *The Incredible Hulk*, and *Wonder Woman*.

Quiet echoes of, "Hush" from everyone, made possibilities of warmth, and love play with the family's emotions. It was the best part of the day, like putting a bow on a gift box of the day.

~ ~ ~ ~ ~

These days, she went to the bedroom, with a can of *Coors Lite*. The tiny TV on the dresser, winked out a rerun of *Sex in the City*. She had softer pillows in the bedroom. She knew his couch pillows, were corduroy.

She wished him mucho discomfort and misery. Simple things pissed them off when they shared time in the house.

He likes windows wide open.

She likes windows shut.

It's rare that a cool breeze,

will bring an iota of cool joy, through the screens.

~ ~ ~ ~ ~

He stares at his suitcase. The sixteen-wheeler is warmed up and ready to roll to West Virginia, as soon as he climbs in. He has a plan. He is going to pick up red flowers at Wal-Mart and present them as a gift of love to the waitress with popcorn curls at the Dixie Truck Stop. He is gonna ask her to quit her job and go on the road with him, right now.

Once gone, he won't have to soul search, and wrestle with infidelity and disappointing his Mom and Dad. This waitress, at the very least, makes him feel something. It has been a long time since his heart has tampered with a plus feeling. He feels like a shit. He can accept being a shit if the waitress holds his dick.

He takes in all the Marlboro gives him and lets out a cloud of smoke the size of a refrigerator door. He wishes his Cinemax hadn't run out of steam.

~ ~ ~ ~ ~

In between breaths, she watches *Scrubs* reruns. If you are over four years old, it's tough to sustain a grin in this house. She hopes he will roll his semi into a fog, filled with lions and tigers, and venereal disease. He hopes to be out of the house spooning up a bucket's worth of truck stop biscuits and gravy. If he'd stayed, she might've tapped into her *bold gene* and said, "We need to talk!"

About the kids,

66

bills,

that woman,

or worse still, the future.

They found refuge, with ears buried in pillows. They both knew post-it notes are the most effective way of *talking*. They're concise, and can be crumpled up, and tossed across the room.

She hears the truck rumble and hum. Doors slam. She knows he will soon be southbound on 57. She lets some of that abandoned peace sneak into her cranium.

Junior has slept with her in the big boat bed. She is changing. She changes the diaper. She changes the sheets of bed. She changes into jeans, and a Reba t-shirt. She decides this is the day to change the locks, so Daddy can't come into the house, with his oily musk, again, without permission.

When she was at Wal-Mart yesterday, she sat with a couple whose pickup—with a mattress in the bed—was stuck in twelve inches of mud. They had desperation sketched into their filthy faces. They sipped small coffees and counted their curled-up cash, on the red tabletop. Only two *Winston's* were left in the soft pack. They stunk like carnival garbage. They referred to each other as fiancées. It was sweet to hear. She purchased their coffees, and sat with them, as she told her story of losing Teddy, and watching her husband, squander away his soul, and wander into gloom.

"Someone is always the asshole. Lock the fuck-head out. Get the money out of the bank. Get a fucking lawyer." said the female fiancé.

She wished she could get really mad. It was a good time to hustle up some rage, but her soul didn't have the taste for it, yet. Was she pissed at her husband, or God? Did she want a leather exterior? She could use a little miracle, even an extra pocket would be something.

~ ~ ~ ~ ~

She got the crew together for breakfast. They filled the table with their precious faces alive with the magic of *Lucky Charms* waiting for the Nestles chocolate, meeting 2% milk, creating the best taste in their tiny worlds. She looked at the simple beauty of their hair, their tiny, busy fingers, and their hopeful bright eyes.

"Can we go to the park?"

"Can we have a picnic?"

"Can we do something that will make us smile?"

She closes her eyes and sees Teddy. He holds a balloon, and runs in circles with all the fun you can pack into a moment. He tells her, all she has to do is to make her kids safe, and have fun.

Keep balloons around.

Don't throw away that big box.

Don't be so sad.

Play in the sandbox.

Play the drums.

I love you Mommy.

~ ~ ~ ~ ~

They arrive at the park. They teeter, they totter, they swing with Skippy faces. It is not perfect there are still skinned knees. Nobody says life is a *good deal*. But Teddy's spirit flows in his veins, like a warm blanket. It keeps the urge to hate off the picnic table.

As Long as You Live in My House

I had this everyday morning ritual. Waking up on the bottom bunk. Sitting up and bumping my head on the top bunk.

IT HURT EVERY SINGLE DAY.

I should have worn a football helmet to bed. The faceguard would also prevent me from spooning an entire box of *Captain Crunch* into my face.

Anyway

Anyhow

Anybody

Any

Any?

I was an eleven-year-old boy forced to get ready for church. I had cousins that weren't forced to attend church. They had to do an act of goodwill instead. Like taking a written note from Aunt Marge, allowing them to purchase extended Winston cigarettes. Nothing of a religious, or spiritual obligation was required from their pre-teen souls. I admit to holding more than just a little bit of jealousy, toward my cousin's faithlessness.

On Sunday mornings I never got my hair dry enough for Dad. I'd trudge out the bathroom. He'd take the towel off my shoulders, and pulsate my scalp, like my head was full of Satan and he could shake him out. I guess a kid needs a rugged drying off.

Echoes of…

"As long as you live in MY house, you're gonna follow MY rules,"

…shook about in my parochial, elementary, thinking department. Along with significant musings like,

'Linda Lloyd sure grew some big bazoombas over the summer, but that didn't work out well for Laura Wells.'

My head needed a recovery period after Dad's spa treatment. My brother, David, was the top bunk border. He had the refinement of most twelve-year-old's. He could beat me up. He DID beat me up! He could make me laugh. He DID make me laugh. A LOT! He owned that extra year, of crude *Southside Chicago* maturity, that some guys, like me, never obtain.

We both lived under the conditions of a paternal, unwritten Joe Doherty lease:

"As long as YOU live in MY house…"

On Sundays, the dot-dot-dot was followed with,

"You WILL go to Mass, DAMMIT!"

Mass at St. Ethelreda was a sour, creepy experience. Stain-glass windows glowingly recreated the final torture house for Jesus Christ. The music sounded like maimed zombies from *Creature Features,* singing songs I'd never hear on WLS.

Ushers shoved long handled baskets in front of your face, that never collected enough money for the bishop to become a cardinal. Repetitive speeches from Father Kill (real name), reminded us that, we're all on Marshall Field escalators heading upstairs for *halos and wings,* and downstairs for *matches and pitchforks.*

Life, after death, downstairs,

did not include hymns, from our organist,

Sister Evelyn Dick,

who specialized in death marches,

on the Hammond organ.

Dad always dreamed of his two boys becoming altar boys; to become closer to this stained glassed institution. David and I always wanted *NOT* to become altar boys. We already knew we did *NOT* want to belong to a tithing system that gleaned eleven per cent of our pocket change popped into cute little envelopes.

David and I were dropped off by Mom, after a partial breakfast of three Hostess powdery donuts, and orange juice. Mom promised us, "Bacon and eggs," if we could just survive 10 a.m. Mass at St. Ethelreda. I guess Mom felt we could be trusted, to be *good little Catholic soldiers*, for an hour.

An hour is a long time to be good.

If left to our own devices, at home, we fought over:

What to watch on TV?

And, who sits in the big black chair?

We'd let the phonograph needle sit on *Born to be Wild* by Steppenwolf, until a parent screamed from the top of the basement stairs, "Turn that damn thing down!" Life was great, if we got more than 35 seconds of maximum RCA volume.

Mom always dropped us off, saying, "Dad is coming with me to the 11:30 Mass." Dad rarely went to 11:30 Mass because he'd miss a half-hour of the Bears game.

Sometimes, I'd stop at the back of the church, and light a candle for a cousin in Viet Nam. Or maybe, I'd hang onto my change, and just sit down.

Sitting was only part of the equation. I always chose an older person, who looked smarter than us. I knelt when he did, sat when he did, and stood when he did. St. Ethelreda's parishioners were better trained than our dog, Missy!

It always amazed me how some old lady, who looked one-hundred-years old, could kneel longer than me. She must practice all week. We were supposed to be, *Born to be MILD* for our souls, so flock members could say, "Those Doherty boys (even though we weren't altar boys) are fine young men, who can behave for short spurts of time."

I don't know which of our butts leaned against the pew seat first, but pretty soon, we were cheating on a kneeling phase of the Mass. We were supposed to kneel in a Catholic group expression of misery. Sister Vivian claimed, "It's a sin to *cheat kneel*." Well, that was what Thursday confession, was all about.

I'd rather say twelve Hail Mary's

than kneel straight up,

with a spiritual posture.

David and I soon relaxed, opened up the hymn book, and pretended to sing. But, while David softly sang a *Tom Jones* song, I was thinking, *What's Up Pussycat*. Then, David whispered, "Let's make Herbie laugh."

I imagined all altar boys, were swept up, in a holy fury of spirituality, but I was wrong. Herbie was the exception to the rule. He was a plump kid, with a perpetual longing to giggle. David locked eyes with Herbie. Then, turning his head sideways, David pretended to jam his middle finger up his nose.

Just as Father Kill finished saying, "It's very important not to hold grudges against one another." We were supposed to kneel again. And that's when Herbie cracked a smile. David, now in full force, tore off a corner of the church bulletin, that advertised *Mr. Concrete* on the back. Sticking the paper in his mouth,

David made a spitball.

Which he launched,

with a green rubber band,

At Herbie.

And missed.

It only flew three rows. And hit a man who thought it was a bug. The parishioner swatted the stale church air, with his fedora. David, Herbie and I were doing our best to sustain brethren laughter. But, although we were not making actual noise, our entire bodies were jiggling like a bowl of red Jell-O.

It was ever so hard to turn holiness on, and off.

I sat for a minute with my hands in prayer. I did not want to do communion. If I wasn't with my parents, I forgot what pew I'd chosen. And I looked stupid searching for my pew, surrounded by dozens of expert pew locaters.

I stayed put.

So did David.

We put the kneelers up,

so other people could get by.

We figured *communion abstainers* should be allowed to sit. We sat and watched one-hundred and seven people go up, and get a wafer that didn't have much taste. People moved in an orderly flow. Communion was a great opportunity to check out girls who usually wore dresses to Mass.

David punched my arm, whenever a female met his, *"She's a fox"* criteria. One old lady walked with a crooked crutch. It was a real struggle for her to walk. David jabbed me and whispered, "Mr. Dillon, Mr. Dillon," just like Chester on *Gunsmoke.* We laughed out loud. The old lady had the same facial hair as Chester, too.

Laura Wells walked by and smiled at one of us. I hoped her smile was targeted at me, and not at David. I smiled back.

Then, my Dad walked by on his way North for communion. He gave us the glare of condemnation. My heart sank to organs below my stomach. We were doomed! Dad looked like Richard Nixon. He got that a lot. Nobody on the planet, not even the Russians, wanted anything to do with Tricky Dick. We didn't either.

Something came over us, and we became angelic for the rest of the Mass. Our sister Diane played the organ on Saturday evening masses. Oh, why hadn't I gone to mass with her yesterday! We waited for father Kill to say those magic words, "The Mass is over, Go in Peace."

I wasn't thinking we were going to experience anything peaceful. Dad was waiting for us at the entrance. I felt the wrath of Joe Doherty would explode like an M-80 inside a watermelon. I knew he was gonna have to use his parental skills.

Dad took us by the scruff of our necks, and guided us into a corner, at the rear of the church, near the candles.

"You boys,

are gonna go,

to the 11:30 mass,

all over again!"

"But, but" said David.

"No Buts!"

We always thought it was funny to hear him say, "No Butts." We sat in different pews for the 11:30 mass. We kneeled like we were one-hundred-year-old ladies. We went to communion because we were hungry. 11:30 mass didn't have any funny stuff about it. It was the perfect punishment, for our crimes and misdemeanors. Dad went home and watched the Bears at noon.

I look back and think, *'My Dad did the best he could. He didn't want us to become parish members of the street corners. He wanted us to have a foundation.'*

The funny thing about writing this story, is that I called my brother to ask about his memory of that Sunday.

He didn't remember it at all!

Funny how something,

so profound

for one person,

can be almost nothing for another.

Bob the Vampire

The truth is, that I am new to this. I still have designs on biscuits and gravy, patty melts, chicken livers, and McDonald's chicken nuggets but, I can't handle them anymore. Gosh, how I miss mornings with Cap'n Crunch.

I've had this rather dramatic diet change to *blood,* ever since I got bit in the neck by a nun.

Yes, a nun.

I had been waiting to volunteer at *St. Brenda's Catholic Church,* when Sister Donna looked me in the eyes. I became a pupil, to pupils. She demanded canned goods for the poor, and I had none. She then asked, "Can I pierce your double chinned neck with my front teeth?"

I thought she was joking so I said, "Ok."

You're supposed to honor nuns.

She led me to a basement pantry and took my soul, as I willingly obliged my neck. I sank, and stared at cans of diced tomatoes, creamed corn and some cans without labels—mystery food if you will.

I fell into a funky drunky sleep.

I woke, I guess, as a vampire, in a pile of uncomfortable boxes of twisted pasta.

I haven't slept since.

You know, I've always been the *Bela Lugosi* fan:

He was scary.

He was ugly.

He was charming…and

I think he had a mild heroin addiction later in life.

Where does one go for instruction for the lurking, blood thirsty dead? Sister Donna was through with me. She was rude. I remember her last words, "You're on your own Bob!" She certainly lost her sense of *Christian Christianity*. I looked at myself the best I could, because some mirrors helped, and others did not. Maybe the good sister thought it was funny to create a 333-pound, civil service, prison guard, vampire dad, who was in the middle of a messy divorce.

Why did she pick me?

How was I going to learn to be a bat, and flutter about? Was I gonna have even more complex faith issues? Was I gonna have to stop going to mass? Was the crucifix gonna make me melt, like a Hershey bar on a summer day?

What about communion? I had better get a library book.

Will this vampire thing cause me to lose weight? Will I need *lite blood*? What will happen if I eat pineapple pizza? Can I still have sex with my wife…well with other women? Can I throw away the *Cialis*? What about bowel movements? It is like being a parent?

There is no manual.

I am claustrophobic, so lying in a coffin will be tortuous. Plus, I never did sign up for a pre-paid burial plan. So, my only realistic option— 'cause I can't kill myself anymore, 'cause I'm dead—is to live my life, and kill, and suck on the blood of convicts at work. Mostly losers, whom other folks are glad to see expired.

I guess I could kill others, but what if somebody I kill, comes back to life? Then, I will not be doing the Christian thing by creating new life, for people who aren't married. So, if I take advantage of my place on the totem pole of life: that of being a prison guard who plays a lot of *computer solitaire,* on my night shift, and kills the occasional bad person, whom, if they lived, would still be in prison 'cause even if I learned the bat metamorphosis skills, I surely wouldn't teach it to a guy, who won't even go to church, even if he could.

God, I would love to have a *beer battered onion ring*.

Being a large man—can I consider myself to be a man? Or, being a large bloodsucking mammal, with a gut, the size of Pittsburgh, I can get ravenous. I could *trance* people with my eyes, and make them *listen up* and *behave*. All the prisoners on my unit are profoundly irrational men with assorted pasts of violence, and inability to control their felonious tempers. Tonight, they're listening to *Abba's* greatest hits and playing *Hungry Hippo,* and *Candyland*, with shitfaced dazed smirks on their convicted faces. They want their turns too.

I ask Wilbur Joyce Johnson to meet me in his cell. I bite him on the calf, through a tattoo—a colorful faded scene, of either the *Eiffel Tower* or *Leaning Tower of Pisa.* I have a hard time stopping drinking his blood, even though it isn't palatable. I'd like some *iced blood* someday, maybe with a slice of lime. Wilbur Joyce is a miserable slug anyway. Prisoners tease him about his middle name, and he pouts. When I leave him, he must be short about thirty-five, 8oz glasses of blood. He looks gaunt.

I give him some *Peach Nehi* from the staff fridge. His last word is, "Thanks!" Then he expires. His tattoo structure looks uneven on his scrawny body. It may be possible, that tattoos spoil the initial taste of blood. It may be possible, that prisoners who pretty much eat dog food, produce blood that tastes like *MD 20/20*. Kind of like having *Budding Beef* instead of sirloin steak.

Here I am, watching my son acting in his school production of Louisa May Alcott's *Little Men.* He performs admirably especially compared to his friend, Atticus, who picks dry skin off of bare feet, while on stage. That won't look good in the Jr. High theatre critique.

It's of some interest to be among mortals. I'm glad I'm not thirsting for Atticus's toes. I have found it possible to include in my new diet; Raisinets, and liver pâté with vegetable flavored Triscuits.

It's easy so far to avoid Sister Donna. I imagine her to have plenty of Diocese menus to choose from for her bloodsucking. You know: old folk who are shut-ins, or people who accidentally lock themselves in confessionals. My mind has wandered, and I have lost the gist of the play. The crowd claps and so does this vampire.

With my arm around my son's eleven-year-old shoulder; I walk through the school hall with a sense of pride.

"Bob!" My wife says with brassy, prissiness.

"Cody," I return with listless passion. I stare at her with my glassy, vacuous eight ball eyes. I look through her *Wal-Mart Optical Center's* transitional lenses, into a fiery suburban soul.

"Take me Bob," she whispers.

It is, at that moment, that my son's wheeled sneakers send him crashing into the school trophy case, and his elbow bleeds. Now, I could help the kid, I could run into Mr. Glassgow's science class and have my way with my separated but willing wife, or I could be late for work. The blood, and the son is too hinky. I command the wife to take care of him. I leave, alone, with juicy fruit on the bottom of my shoe. I wonder where one might buy a cape, in a dark color.

Being a walking dead guy is weird. One day I need a handkerchief, and one day I don't. One day, hemorrhoidal tissue spotting is a major issue and the next day I can safely sit on a fence post if I feel the urge. I look up. I see a busty fast walking woman, with two Basenjis, her iPod earphones loudly playing a version of *Take a walk on the wild side* by William Shatner. I imagine her blood to be tainted by Shatner—whom I suspect is an Episcopalian Vampire. I don't know for sure. Although it's always a temptation, to drink anonymous public blood; it seems a safer lot in non-life to keep chiseling into the tattoos of my prison drones.

The prisoners do little other than exist on my tax dollar. But I have to remember that the salary, to pay me, comes from taxes too. So, am I saving my state and county and country by killing these jailbirds? Or does my *forever* hunger for blood sucking correctional activities, somehow distort the bumpy road of justice in an unethical Blagojevich administration? This is above my pay scale to answer. I ought to run it by my union steward.

I need to confess. Well, not to really confess, but tell a priest about killing cons and not feeling bad about it.

I go to a different church. Something about the Holy Perpetual Crosses Catholic Church is too much to bear.

I stand in line, in the dark cathedral. I look at the crucifix, and find I can stare and stare with only a mild side effect, of a need to scratch behind my knees. I half expect I will melt, or run out screaming *bloody scrutiny*.

Anyway, there's a young woman wearing a *Foghat* t-shirt in front of me. *What kind of sinning has she done*? I hope her sins are brief, so I won't have to wait.

The dark door opens. It's an upright, wider coffin. I take some comfort in this. A little screen opens, and a male voice says, "I'll be right back son."

"OK," I say. It's either a bathroom break, a need for a cool drink of unholy libation, or he's going to return, with a wooden stake to thrust in my upper gut.

Along, with guilty thoughts. I imagine the priest needs Advil or Tylenol to continue in this world of constant forgiveness.

The light comes back on. "Make it snappy my son! There's a long line, of *long in the tooth* seniors, who just got back from Paradise Casino. I could be here for hours. What's your sin?"

"I killed some prisoners. I became a vampire, and I got hungry, and sucked too much blood. But I'm not sure if I was just doing my job. Or I was just hungry."

"Bless your soul my son. You're not a killer. You just have a nasty, schizophrenic evil condition."

"You think so?" I ask.

"Yes, I know so. Say the *rosary* seventeen times and don't eat pink meat tomorrow."

"Okay."

I sit in a white wicker rocker in my garage apartment. I can stomach stewed tomatoes, with Splenda this evening. So far, killing a prisoner is an every other night *adventure stain* on my so-called life. I can't picture a motion picture about my life. My life would sputter and spit, even before Sister Donna's chomp on my neck.

Why? Because I stopped trying. I stopped doing anything, except operate a complicated remote at home or babysitting caught criminals with limited sadistic vitality. I always promised my kid, Disney World, but never came through.

Every kid deserves a ride of the tilt-a-whirl. A chance to eliminate vomit on your father's lap while you both scream for rotating distance.

That's how I formed a squishy-smelly bond, with my own father. Maybe I can sue the school for the trophy incident? Use that money to buy a Florida trip? I promise to be a better dad if I win a lawsuit.

Back to work. It's time for an annual evaluation. I always don't like it. Eugene Loverde, my boss, has a nose like a light bulb globe. It has distinguished bumpy continents, fleshy pimply seas and deep bewildering nostrils. Glasses rest on the honker today. His ruddy eyes, that believe they have seen it all, finally meet my newer, shark like eyes.

"You, Bob, are doing a great job! I don't know how you control these bastards, and have them playing in *Candyland* tournaments? But you do it somehow. I have a letter here signed by Governor Blagojevich giving you a *commendation.* You keep doing what you're doing Bob. Keep playing that computer solitaire too, I don't give a hoot."

"OK." I retort. I think about sucking the boss's blood, but decide against it. I fear nasal transference.

Every other night. Convict *Rocky Lee Lickspittle* does his usual routine, of puffing up his tiny, red pillow, and reading *Rod McKuen* poetry, before hitting the hay. I open his cell door, and sit next to him on his bed. All 333 lbs. of me desires a midnight snack. Rocky doesn't have any tattoos to sink my teeth into, but he does have a kind of painful cellulitis, gangrene thing happening to his right foot.

I don't think anyone will notice puncture marks in purple skin.

It's tough to get a lot of blood, and I can taste the Coumadin he's taking. Yuck! I won't drink all the blood. I will allow him to live. Rocky will be my pet convict. Maybe he can help put away Candyland boards.

Eugene returns to the cell block later, with a copy of my evaluation. I play red queen on black king, and nibble on a Triscuit with liver pâté, Eugene left me. Lickspittle survived.

It was about that time to do laundry. I wish I could have put Lickspittle in my pocket so he could fold my XXXL clothes. However, it would stink of unethical behavior, to kidnap the body and soul of Lickspittle and become his master of the Laundromat. I should read up on my union manual.

The wind kind of blows me to Ron's Laundromat. It seems kind of beneath me, to have to actually do laundry. But I do. Otherwise, I will have to purchase new socks, and underwear. I can watch a very undramatic concentrated soap opera, of my clothes tumbling, or I can watch a tiny *Emerson TV,* that's trying ever so hard to retain color.

The TV commercials all focus on consolidating my last 15 years of mistakes, into one fine-tuned, carefully put together, weekly payment of $39.95. The TV crawlers hint at the possibility, of someone having killed on older fella in room *17D,* of the *Do-Si-Do nursing home.* The victim was apparently out of blood, out of cigarettes, and out of luck.

The Republican coroner says, "I've never seen anything like it." He doesn't want to do an autopsy, because they're so messy and expensive. He wants to go home. So, he does.

Newscaster, *Meredith Merideth* reports, "A Honduran assistant Director of nursing, states that a figurine of St. Anthony, spoke to her of a blubbery nun leaning over the victim's neck, and walking off, with a blood-soaked face!"

There's a *dragnet* out searching for Sister Donna.

Father Dick Peter is interviewed, on the steps of *St. Brenda's Catholic Church.* He finds it refreshing, to have nuns blamed for something. But it's hard to believe any Catholic could do something hateful. I can't help, but feel some angst, "Darn that nun."

My thoughts are trying to think, where I will wear a cape if I get one? I really want to do the bat thing.

Once, when I was 13, I killed a bat, after it fell from a shutter. I poured lighter fluid on it, and lit it up. It flew into an old lady's house.

She had 76 cats.

The fiery bat burned her house down.

I was forgiven for that in confession.

I have a parent teacher conference, for my kid tomorrow. The phone rings in the garage apartment. "Hello?"

"Hi Dad. Don't forget teacher conference tomorrow."

"OK." And both phones hang up.

I can think of little other than wanting to rove through night skies as a bat. Of course, I'd rather have vision, over radar as a bat.

Sunshine pass away the limp images of last night's noir. Above the steel wool pad on the sill of the window over the kitchen sink is a bat nibbling through the screen. Seemingly, it asks in *raspy mouse cade*nce to allow it in. The itchy soliloquy ends with flight to a frying pan, with a loose handle through a dark spot in front of the generic cereals where a pool of smoke and the aroma of death dust and fart extinguish into a naked—let's say 256 lb. Caucasian non-exercising woman.

It is the evil Sister Donna!

I bring her my Black & Decker terry cloth robe which she accepts.

She puts it on, and ties it with militant Catholic grace.

The TV screams at us with continuous reruns of the nursery home carnage. "I've had a long night Bob. Wonder if I can stay awhile? Maybe watch *Who Wants to Be A Millionaire*?"

The more I look at her, the more she looks like a female Boris Yeltsin.

"Sure.

Stay Sister.

Stay as long as you like."

We both smoke Old Gold 100's and allow TV to do with it, what it does. It's hard to imagine what vampires did, to kill time, before cable TV.

A knock on the door leads me to thinking, *maybe we was gonna be goners? Perhaps a crew of TV evangelists with broken bats as stakes will pound through our chests.* But it was a dry-cleaning zombie bringing a finely pressed nun-outfit with steel-toed black shoes.

"Pay the man," directs the sister.

The zombie stands with hands out. A chunk of ear slides to his collar bone. He only has one good eyebrow.

"Can you take a check"? I ask.

I write a check and carefully record it on a dinner napkin. I still share this account with my wife, and truth be told; this check is gonna bounce. My current balance is $6.66. The zombie drives away in a rusty Pinto.

The vampire sister trudges to the pantry, and changes into her nun regalia, right in front of *Aunt Jemima, Capn' Crunch* and *Charlie the Tuna*. She walks back, and grabs my exemplary work evaluation, complete with the letter of commendation from Gov. Blagojevich.

"Nice," she says.

"Thank you, sister."

"I got one of these too." She says. "I'm marketing manager of the Do-Si-Do nursing home. It's owned by the Governor's mother's best friend's son. I've been killing DNR patients right before they're Medicaid eligible, and you Bob—you're saving the governor's associates money, by killing too."

85

"Yeah." I say.

"Darn that St. Anthony." Says sister. "I'm gonna hafta get a new means of livelihood or deadhood."

"Yeah. I thought St. Anthony only helped find lost stuff."

"Maybe we can be partners. Maybe work a little closer to the governor."

"Is he one of us too?" I ask.

"He used to be. Something about his hair spray changed him into something much different than us."

"Oh. Can you teach me, that bat metamorphosis thing?" I ask.

"No."

"You know, our prison chaplain is scheduled to retire, maybe you can take his spot. I'll share *Rocky Lee Lickspittle* with you too."

"That'd be cool. Those nursing home residents are on 14 different drugs, it makes the blood taste queasy."

"I know what you mean," I say.

And we smoke and watch *Millionaire* until I have to go to the parent-teacher conference.

Dear Me

Once, after months of frustration, after months of listening to the tenant, over my ceiling stomp on my subsidized efficiency atmosphere, with stiletto heels, digging and dancing, to untender music, that one could march to a death march. I have decided to go upstairs, knock and complain.

But first, I'm going to finish this chicken and cheese Hot Pocket and write a letter to my friend Betty. Her real name is Alicia, but I call her Betty. She calls me Beverly.

The microwave is both friend, and foe of the Hot Pocket. Nothing can ever get so fiery hot as the cheesy stuff. Once I burned my lip on one. I wrote a letter to the Hot Pocket Company to complain and they sent me 101 coupons for free Hot Pockets. I tried to give my Dad a coupon, but he said, "How can you eat those things"?

I've never said *that phrase* to him! Especially when he eats gross sardines out of the can. God never intended a bunch of minnow sized fish to be entombed in oil in a can you could put in your pocket. Has anyone ever tried to bring a can of sardines, through airport security? I know they don't have a sardine Hot Pocket yet. Maybe Dad would come around if they did?

~ ~ ~ ~ ~ ~ ~ ~ ~ ~ ~ ~ ~ ~ ~ ~

Dear Betty,

I'm sending extra blank paper. I have a hard time reading the bottom of your letters, because you have this tendency to make your letters, and words very tiny, and they all seem to hafta commingle, and congregate into the righthand corner of the letter.

Sometimes I wish I had a big magnifying glass, that police detectives use,

so I can make out the righthand corner of her letters. I have to wonder,

if people who wrote letters during the depression, had this issue too.

I am also including a check for $1.08, so you can go to the dollar store, and buy 80 sheets of loose-leaf paper. Or, if you feel that wasting paper is sinful, just do whatever you want.

I did make out in your last letter, that you broke a toe. You didn't say which toe. I was curious, because I broke my middle left toe in 2004, when I fell down four stairs. So, it's nice to have something in common, even if it is an excruciating thing.

My dad is tired of being my representative payee, for my Social Security money. He turns his phone off now. He said, I was calling him in the middle of the night wanting "silly stuff". Well, if silly stuff is Chuck Norris endorsed stuff, I hardly think Mr. Norris would do that. His TV show was cancelled, and everyone needs to make a buck.

I did make it to church. It was a bit too religious for me, if you know what I mean. I am sorry about your daughter's arrest. I don't think they put people in jail for bad checks anymore, since I got my debit card.

Hugs & Love,
Beverly

~~~~~~~~~~~~~~~~

I used to have a boyfriend. He lived with me, and didn't do much of anything. He liked the food channel and wanted me to get a nudie channel, but I told him, "I can expose my tits to you, for much less than $12.95 a month!"

He really liked his Pringles. He wouldn't share the Pringles. He really didn't bring a single Pringle into our relationship.

I think of him as my subsidized boyfriend.

His name was Matt.

Matt went upstairs to tell the tenant to be quiet. Matt's ears were bleeding when he came downstairs. He packed his dirty clothes into a Glad trash bag and left. I never saw him again. Drips of *ear blood* still mark the tile hallway outside. The blood came out of my carpet with a mixture of vinegar, Dawn and salt.

I'm going to do something about the guy upstairs. The police knocked on the tenant's door and then they went back to their squad car, and fought for more urban democracy. My manager is at this 367-4441 number, and is aware of the problem.

I ordered a movie on Netflix. It must have gotten lost in the mail. Getting the mail can be a good part of my day. Sometimes I write to Mom.

Mom has boobs as big as adult human heads, so her neck hurts.

Mom lives in Arkansas. She has a boyfriend, Art, who takes her to a dog track.

Art has a pond right on his property. Art says I can come down, and fish at his pond. I have a hard time picturing myself fishing at the pond. My skin is sensitive to sun, and I can't get excited about worms and bobbers.

It'd be nice to compare my cable TV with Art's dish TV though.

Mom says Art can't bring himself to say, "I love you."

~~~~~~~~~~~~~~~~

Dear Mom,

I'm using my second to last stamp to mail this. I have to save my other stamp in case of emergency. The people upstairs still make tons of night noises. Sometimes, I wish a tornado would swoop their apartment away, and of course, leave mine.

I have a new picture on my wall of Jesus. I took down the Hustler art that Matt left. If I ever have a boy; I'm going to name him after a big city like Chicago, or Boston, or Orleans. I am not currently pregnant, although the cashier at Wal-Mart thought I was.

I got more hot pockets. I only have 18 coupons left. I never tire of the breakfast Hot Pocket. Matt left his Scooby-Doo slippers. I sometimes think he'll come back for my love, and not those slippers. He had big feet. I kind of sponsored Matt's inability to have any ambition, while he was here. It's okay.

I hope Art is Okay. I'm sorry to hear about his erectile dysfunction. There are lots of men with nice sweaters on TV, who get help from doctors. Matt had a very alert penis.

Please write to Dad and tell him to send me more money. It is not as easy as it was.

Love & Hugs,

~ ~ ~ ~ ~ ~ ~ ~ ~ ~ ~ ~ ~ ~ ~

Dear Beverly,

I am also down to 2 stamps. I will mail this to you. I really can't, or shouldn't contact your father. The order of protection is still in effect, but when it is lifted next October, I will write him a thoughtful letter. I never meant to run over his left foot.

Art is doing good. He asked again, if you would like to fish in the pond. He seems to like people he has never met. Someday you two will meet, and then we will see. Tell your father, that the seeds of the milk thistle plant, may serve as a remedy for his liver ailments.

I hope the situation with your *loud* neighbor works itself out. I think you should try *eharmony*, that's how I met Art. I think you still have my Harlan Coben book. Can you mail it to me?

Love and Hugs,

Mom

~ ~ ~ ~ ~ ~ ~ ~ ~ ~ ~ ~ ~ ~ ~

I keep putting off going upstairs. Sometimes the noises start at 10:30 at night, when I'm watching Golden Girls. Sometimes, *Bea Arthur* sounds like my Mom's brother, Keith. The noise is loud, heavy metal music, and it sounds like somebody is re-arranging the furniture. I have not changed the furniture at all since I moved in, except when all the fish died. I put the aquarium in the bathroom. It would be nice to get fish again, someday.

I guess I could always move back with Dad, but he complains I use too much toilet paper. And his dog, *Sneaky*, has moved into my old room.

But 16 hours a day of efficiency residence is pretty good, pretty good. Dad didn't keep his silverware real clean either; who needs more germs? Not me!

~~~~~~~~~~~~~~~~~

Dear Beverly,

I hope this letter finds you in a good mood. Jeopardy is on TV. I watch Jeopardy because my Mother always watches it. It is a hard show.

Thanks for the check. I will buy loose-leaf paper. I have a dollar store close by. My broken toe is the middle toe, of the left foot. It only hurts now, if I kick something hard. It is nice to have something in common with you.

I have problems also with a neighbor. He and his wife make love, in the place above me. Every time I hear them go at it; I miss my first husband, Shorty.

Oh well, my priest is coming by, to give me one of those wafer things. I look forward to hearing from you.

Hugs and kisses,

Betty

~~~~~~~~~~~~~~~~~

The noises are worse than ever tonight. It's like a 16-wheel truck touring through our building. Snow covers the town's lawns and sidewalk. There's a boom-boom, or a boo-boo, or maybe a boom-boo, that happens above me in the tenant's place. There is still music pounding, and loosening screws in my George Foreman grill.

I can't hear the thuds of a ceiling dance, with the devil anymore. I wrap my body in my terry clothed robe, and slip-on Matt's Scooby-Doo slippers. I have a sense of curiosity, and purpose, like the time I looked up *salacious* in the dictionary.

I trudge upstairs. The door is open. Two guys with handguns, lie on the floor. One guy has a winter vest, with a hoody—he's twitching ticks of consciousness. The other guy is wearing Tighty-whities. He looks like his life has no more twists or shouts.

"Do you mind if I turn down the stereo?" I ask. Neither guy seems to care, so my dog slippers and I walk over to the stereo. They are listening to a CD, called the Spiders Bladder. There's a red gym bag on the floor with money in it.

"Do you guys mind if I take this bag?"

The two guys again, have no response.

I go back to my apartment.

I notice Matt's Scooby slippers now have blood on them. I walk them outside and run back into my building in my socks. One sock is black, one is purple.

In no time at all snow covers up my *near the dumpster* footprints. I must have been confused because I don't bring down my own garbage with my slippers. There are a lot of Hot Pockets wrappers in the trash too.

The gym bag with the money sits on a chair. It's a really bright red *St. Louis Cardinal* bag. I am a Cub fan, because my Uncle Keith was a Cub fan, and when I was little, he gave me a Cubbies monkey that had Don Kessinger's autograph on the rear end. Last year on voting day; I saw Uncle at the polls, and he asked for it back. I lied and said, I lost it.

Actually, it's in a plastic bag, under the sink next to the Drano.

There appears to be a lot of money in the bag. One twenty with a deceased president's face staring up at me. I wonder if this dead president realized his sensuality toward young women when he stared with such abandoned passion. I don't feel like counting money right now.

Joan Rivers is trying to sell me a unique extra sensationally sparkly earring. If I buy one; I'll get one free. I've never bought nothing from the channel before. Dad said this channel sucks. Dad likes sports, and news, and documentaries about Russian mail order brides. It's a temptation.

I'm thinking a lot about upstairs. I'm waiting for a bunch of cops to stomp up the stairs and do CSI stuff. I think about calling the police. I also think those guys upstairs have been very uncivilized, even rude being so boisterous to me and my ceiling.

One of the best things to do, is get out my number 2 pencil, and write a letter to myself. If it's a good letter, I will go to Kinko's and copy it for Mom, and Betty.

~~~~~~~~~~~~~~~~

Dear Me,

   Once, on an episode of Gilligan's Island, they kept saying the word, preposterous. I never looked up that word. I have lived a long time, with some regret.

   Now I have come to a place where, if I was driving a Hovercraft, I would either swerve, or stop and go. Dad says, *stop and go* is a receiver's route in football. If I share this situation with somebody else, they may tell me to go to church, and before you know it, I'd give the church some money, and a minister might fall in love with me. Hmmmm.

You know I might go someplace. A place to consider what to do. I have never told nobody; not even me before, that, if my life becomes—I fear to say—preposterous, I will take a smelly old Greyhound, to the Wisconsin Dells. I like wave machines. Some folk may think this is nutty, but it's been my far-flung dream, for a while.

There's a poem that talks about making a *path* decision, or maybe that was something about going west, while you was young. I often wonder if Harlan and Kurt Cobain were related. Someday, I will write a book about my life. I don't know who will read it, but somebody keeps buying those Harry Potter mysteries. If they make a movie out of my life; I would like Audrey Hepburn to come to life, gain 37 pounds, and act like me.

Anyway, me, I am getting off of the railroad track of my duties. I can share with myself, that I have to go number 2 pretty soon too. So, me, I will take the cursed Cardinal bag, and stick it in my Cub suitcase, and I will have my entire body, bussed to the Dells.

Hopefully, when I get back to town, the upstairs tenants will have been totally evicted, evacuated, and hopefully ejected to heaven, where they can just try to make noise with clouds. Thanks for everything me. I love me, most of the time.

Sincerely,

Me

~~~~~~~~~~~~~~~~~

I have turned Joan Rivers off. My friend Betty says, "Plants like TV." I have an African violet, that doesn't like to have its leaves dampened. If I was a plant, I'd watch that Bounty Hunter show. With lots of papered president's, in my purse, I call Corky's cab, and as the backdoor slams; I enter, and enjoy the world of Floyd Stutzman, cab driver–extra-ordinaries.

Since we aren't in a hurry, we go through a car wash. I don't mind. A carwash can rinse off your car's sins, if that is what you desire. When Floyd looks back at me, I notice frizzy hairs have grown in ears. He talks to me about his old job of painting Indian art on Frisbees and hand saws.

I give him 76 cents as a tip. I don't like giving tips. No one ever gives me pocket change. Floyd looks at me, as if our friendship is over. It is kind of over.

I would hafta go to Chicago first, then Rockford, and then Wisconsin Dells. I have a taste for a ham and cheese Hot Pocket. I thirst for Wisconsin cheese curds. I think about all that money stuck in my Cubs suitcase.

My Dad started saying this saying, "It's all good."

I never know what that means, because he is always pissed off.

When I was little I always; said, "Here's Johnny!" And people laughed, until I said it seven times. I can't see Dad being a man who would sit in a big pool, and wait for the waves to come.

~~~~~~~~~~~~~~~~

Dear Betty,

I am writing this with a green felt pen. I found it on the bathroom floor, at the Greyhound station in Chicago. I have recently come into some money, but I can't tell you anything about it. Why do you think my breasts never developed very much? I am taking a vacation to the Dells.

I want to sit in the indoor pool, and feel artificial warm Wisconsin waves, caress my buttocks. Maybe I'll send you a postcard? I hope the hotel sells stamps. If I can, I will write you every day – like a travel journal.

The bus just passed a Crispy Crème donut shop. I don't know what a Wisconsin Dell is, but there must be a lot of them. Minnesota has 1,000 lakes. I find that hard to believe. There is this guy with a computer watching an R rated movie, with boobs, and his little boy is watching too. What is this world coming to Betty?

Hugs and love,

Beverly

~~~~~~~~~~~~~~~~~
</div>

The hotel is so nice. My room is right by the elevator, the ice machine, and a roomed couple, who praise God whenever they have intercourse, which upsets their pagan German Shepard; apparently.

I start counting the money in the bag. I was going to roll my body on the cash, on the bed but then I thought about money germs. I decide to count it later. The dishwasher at Denny's smiled at my table's direction. He had a smirk. The chlorine treated waves surpass my glorified expectation.

I watch a porno movie. I decide never to order thick crust pizza again. I have now been gone four days. I want to go home. I wish I was Samantha Stevens, not because of Dick York or Dick Sargent, but because

I could rotate my nose 90 degrees, and I could be home. I will write mom, and tell her I am on a trip with a ski club.

~ ~ ~ ~ ~ ~ ~ ~ ~ ~ ~ ~ ~ ~ ~ ~

```
Dear Mom
     I am on a trip with my ski club. I have not
busted any bones. Tell Art, I say Hi! Tell me what you
want for your Valentine's Day.
                         Love & Hugs,
                         Beverly
```

~ ~ ~ ~ ~ ~ ~ ~ ~ ~ ~ ~ ~ ~ ~ ~

The other side of a postcard is a color picture of a squirrel with skis on his bottom feet. The postcard would make a nice addition to anyone's refrigerator door. I picture letters from Mom, and Betty, and Comcast, when I get home. Life is funny, your tummy can get so happy on a Hot Pockets diet, and then Denny's makes you have to go to the bathroom a lot.

I am sitting next to an Asian man. The bus is full. He has headphones on. He is playing a game with tiny soldiers on his tiny phone. If I had flown to the Dells, I would have had to pay extra for my Cub luggage. $20 dollars? What is this world coming to?

My Dad used to have a bong. It reminds him of happier times. I hope the bus doesn't hit a deer, or if it does, I hope it is an old deer and not a young feller. I never catch the Asian man staring at my knees. Maybe he is gay.

~ ~ ~ ~ ~ ~ ~ ~ ~ ~ ~ ~ ~ ~ ~ ~

```
Dear Me,
     I can't wait to get back home, and go back to my
cherished routines. TV is always better at home, and I
don't think I have bed bugs. I'm not sure why I even
```

brought that up. I just want my life back the way it was.

I think my mattress is from Dads Aunt Anita. I could buy a newer one now. Now, my life is gonna be quiet, the tenants are probably in a drawer in the morgue. The manager is probably shampooing the carpets. Probably a nice quiet immigrant, from a quiet nation will move in.

The nice thing about writing to myself besides refocusing on the important things, is that I do not need a stamp. I'm pretty sure Mom will not believe in my ski club story, but I think a little bit of falsifying, brings out juicy mystery, and Mom reads Harlan Coben books so let it be, God. What will I do with the money? I will keep it Cubbed up in that bag.

I will try to buy some Hot Pockets lite, for when Lent comes up. Hear that God? I'm gonna be good for Lent, except for Fridays, 'cause there ain't a fishy Hot Pocket yet. So *please, and thank you* too, God, for the opportunity to live my life as I am accustomed. Lord knows. You know. A girl can use a break.

Love you,

Me

~~~~~~~~~~~~~~~~

Dear Mom

I am back from my ski club meeting in Wisconsin. We skied in between big and small Dells. I don't think I will ski much more, because I quit the ski club because all the other members are in their 70's.

I haven't read your letter yet. Do you know that it could cost me $2.92, to send the Harlan Coben book back to you? Why don't you go to Goodwill, and buy a used book? You are driving me crazy about that, and I have nothing more to say.

Love and hugs,

Beverly

P.S. Give Art my love

~~~~~~~~~~~~~~~~

Dear Betty,

I had a good time at the Dell's. I almost met a dishwasher at Denny's, but it wasn't meant to be. There was no exuding of sexual sparks.

It is good to be home. Someday, I will tell you the whole story, about how I got a whole bunch of money in a funny way. I am sharing too much. I am sorry to hear of your hamster's untimely bout with gout. I'm sure with our prayers, and your loving hands, the little pooper will be ok.

I don't hear a lot of noise from upstairs. I feel funny about things up there, but like Dad says, "Be careful what you ask for."

Love and hugs,

Beverly

~~~~~~~~~~~~~~~~

I can hear my TV without hearing big noises from upstairs. I feel a little like an apprentice criminal. I wonder if I should go upstairs. First, I am gonna warm up this Salisbury steak Hot Pocket. It has a funny taste. I think you call it freezer burn. You would think another person in the building, would see me in the hall and say, "Hey, Beverly, the guy upstairs is dead." People don't talk so much though. They don't like me, or they don't talk American.

It seems like a job to lift each foot up the stairs. I can still hear the Spider's Bladder music in the foyer. I push open the door and much to my dismay, the guys are still dead, but now dead in a stinkier way. I close the door. It's not my business. I decide, right then and there to watch this Golden Girls episode, even though I have the DVD, and I've seen it 9 times already.

~~~~~~~~~~~~~~~~~~

Beverly,

You have acted like a little brat or since you went to Wisconsin—a big brat. I can't help it.

You sound different. Maybe you should take some St. John's wart medicine. I hear it makes peoples souls, soar with gritty happiness. You don't sound like yourself. Art is concerned too, even though he has not talked to you.

The reason that the Harlan Coben book is important to me, is because that's the book I bought at the hospital, when you had your appendix out. Some of your *throw up* is on page 211. Please respect an old woman's wishes and send it to me. Here is $5 in cash. Please have fun with the extra 2 bucks.

Art needs me right now.

I love you, bunches.

<div align="center">Love,

Mom</div>

Mr. Exciting Guy

The fan makes a lot of noise as it propels around, and around, bringing cool air downwards onto his hairy back. He drifts into a beautiful sleep, after having just made love to his sweetheart. He hears the shower and thinks about getting out of bed, and rinsing the smell of sex off his body.

But it's so comfortable just soaking up the warmth of this comforter, and dreaming about the passion he'd felt just minutes ago. He can hear Letterman chattering away about the Top Ten ways to pronounce Barrack Obama. He smiles, reaches for the remote, and turns off the TV.

It's probably his last task of the day, or perhaps she may come back to bed and want to be held. He can do that. He's ready for her to be smelling like a flower, and crawling into his chest, and being so close, that the two of them feel like one.

And he's asleep.

Slam. A sharp boom of pain hits him in the head. He looks up. She's dressed in a skimpy, pink negligee—a gift from him. She holds a long, red handled spade, he'd bought her last spring.

She raises it again to strike him. He freezes with fear as he sees it coming at him. Only this time it strikes the fan, and a wooden blade falls on the bed. She raises the shovel again. He gets out of bed, wrestles the spade from her, and throws her on the bed.

He grabs his jeans, runs downstairs, through the living room, and out the front door. He turns around, looks through the screen door, and sees her beautiful self, with shovel in hand, and his blood and hair, on the end of its shining surface.

A cold stream of blood trickles down his back. He feels his head, then looks at his hand and sees more blood and loose hairs. He pulls his jeans on, and runs down the street.

He rustles out of sleep, and leans over to drink some warm water out of his glass. He can't seem to stop this damn dream from reoccurring. He feels the back of his head. There's no blood, and no evidence of a spade having dug a hole into his head.

It's relief.

A relief, for sure.

It's a satisfaction that he was just emotionally terrorized, and not physically traumatized. The water feels good in his mouth. The escape into sleep, from the million thoughts of her—good and bad—had been welcome.

But it's hard to acknowledge that the *bad*, outweighed the really *good* times.

How many times could she accuse him of seeing other women? How many times could she tell him, "You're hiding things from me!" How many of his old friends has he lost, through this relationship?

Oh, she was so beautiful, and so loving most of the time. But the daily pain, and anxiety, is like a knife twisting in his heart. Another day of thoughts of her—good and bad—can't be good. He looks at the clock; 2pm and reaches over for a bottle of Ambien. He swallows a couple, hoping to sleep more of this day away.

He has just broken up from a relationship, with a very attractive, crazy woman. His stomach churns, like it's full of cheese curds. Pain travels up his GI tract, like an oral colonoscopy.

He longs for the attractive, crazy woman.

Or tries to love again.

It would be nice to test drive a new face, and body.

Or at least kick her tires.

He left her, not for some meaningless reason, like her favorite movie was *Starsky and Hutch*, but because she threw darts at his heart, and the passion in his heart began to ooze out.

His therapist told him how she suffocated him.

He imagined himself walking about with a *down pillow* strapped to his face.

Now, he is never hungry and never interested in a thing. Booze and cigarettes are welcome friends, of possible self-induced destruction, of his body.

She has shredded his soul.

He survives.

He recalls her rants, her never being able to trust him, no matter what he did.

So, it is after all, a Friday night and the laundry needs to be done. She never sorted his socks anyway, and true love is a woman who will sort his socks, roll them up in playful balls, and stuff them in the warmth of the dresser drawer.

And you know, it's a remote possibility, but perhaps love might be found at the Laundromat, between the change machine, and the filthy sink. There's always that.

Not much chance of finding the *love of his life* in this apartment!

It's only been two weeks since he moved into this clean, modern apartment, on the ground floor. Despite art posters—with multicolored thumbtacks holding them up—and rarely seen family photos on the walls, the mood of the place has changed from a *new hope* to a *sensible, depressed ambiance*. A cardboard box holds up his new color TV, and an old desk holds up an antiquated, but still useful computer.

He likes his cable TV.

He likes TV.

The TV and computer are his tools, to combat what to do the other sixteen hours a day, he has to work. Perhaps he'll buy a couch one day, or something that isn't purchased at a garage sale, or thrift shop. He really should get something new, to pep up his sorry ass.

He owns the plastic hamper. It was his, and not hers after he moved out. He finds dirty socks under a comforter on a futon mattress, he's been sleeping on. He finds towels that need to be addressed, in the bathroom. He finds an incredibly dirty washrag, hanging over the faucet in the kitchen. It has that putrid kind of smell, and wonders if he should pitch it, or wash it. He throws it in his hamper. He finds sweatshirts without sweat, and shirts with latte stains. All the clothes, and for that matter, everything in the apartment has that special *Paul Mall Ultralight* scent.

He has that going for him.

The TV blares an *ABC* show, with Regis Philbin's female, morning partner. A laugh track produces the recorded laughs of people, who might be the same people, who laugh for Bob Denver and Alan Hale Jr. on *Gilligan's Island*.

Mr. Exciting Guy leaves the apartment with the TV on. He leaves the sad two-bedroom apartment, with ideas of hiring a cleaning woman, to make it look like it did, when he moved in. Or at least make it better.

Of course, it's dark and rainy on this Friday night. The windshield wipers struggle with indecision. Should they swipe intermittently? Or should they swipe like a real man?

Real man swipes, prevail.

Four people are smoking cigarettes in the mist outside the Victory Laundromat. They slide their asses against a wet Oldsmobile. They appear to be talking to someone. Some allow him to hear one sided conversations from their mouths into tiny silver cellphones. One woman insists the caller put the baby on the line. She tells her baby that she loves her. I wonder what the baby thinks about that. The rest of the auditory stimulation comes from Al Green swooning from overhead speakers telling all the laundry doers that he's tired of being alone.

Al Green competes with little itsy-bitsy color TV's strapped to pedestals so none of us washer or dryer people have any wicked ideas of absconding with them into the dank night. One TV shows Raymond Burr reprise his Perry Mason role. Perry is telling the judge that the jury must be sequestered.

Six quarters, and three washing machines.

He jams the quarters in, and sorts *darks and lights* as if the world gives a flying fuck if his colors get tinted. However, at forty-seven years of age, he discovers the courage to wear underwear that isn't always white. He did it for the crazy, attractive former girlfriend.

He recalls some of what he liked about this crazy, attractive woman. She always told him that she loved him. He liked to hear that. She allowed him to kiss her all over, to stroke her hair, and listen when he told her about his day. But he had to edit his day, in case another woman had spoken to him.

She loved to kiss, and engage in long passionate lovemaking. She made him drinks, and lit his smokes. She said she loved the music he put on his cd player.

The lights turn off on washing machine number 19. He gets one of those aluminum, holey gurneys with the squiggly wheels. He unloads clothes from the washer and makes a deposit of *wet darks* to dryer number 23. He's fascinated to see the new technology of dryers, counting off the seconds, and minutes of drying time. He watches each quarter drop into the dryer, and count off seven minutes. Seven less minutes in the Exciting Guy's life ticks off, as his holy blue jeans wrestle his grey Duke t-shirt, into an ultimate spin, and final surrender.

The dryers signal what might be the end of the evening for him. How can he top the exciting evening, after the clothes get folded? Oh, if only former crazy, girlfriend would walk up in her pink negligee, and roll up the socks for him.

Perry Mason is wrapping up another case. The defendant sits in satisfaction, as a man from the back of the courtroom squeals out his guilt. Monotone Perry Mason insists to the judge, that the defendant, be released.

As he's leaves the Laundromat, Mr. Exciting Guy wonders if many people stay to watch the end of TV programs, after their laundry work is done. Carole King crackles through overhead speakers, about some louse named *Smackwater Jack*. He pushes his butt against the door into the night.

This 47-year-old decides to go to a bar. He actually bellies up to the bar. So far, a successful evening, and a task completed. He knows he will not have the strength to put his clothes away when he gets home.

He lights up a smoke. His smoke joins a larger cloud that hovers over an early night group of alcohol consumers. The bartender has piercings in her eyebrows and a nose ring. She's dressed in a bright red, retro pant suit. He orders a rum and diet coke. She asks if he wants a lime with that. He nods. This is the first time all day that another person has spoken to him.

Damn.

Nobody even called on the phone, to sell him a different phone plan.

He imagines if his former crazy girlfriend were here, he'd have to be on his best behavior. He'd look away if a pretty female walked by. She'd say she dressed up for him. And did not deserve the disrespect he might show…if he glanced at another female! She'd say she deserved better.

He'd have to devote all his attention on her.

Maybe escape a few minutes, to check the score on the TV.

He'd act uninterested, if a cheerleader appeared on screen.

The key was to devote himself to her, with all his mind, body and soul, not show any sign of being human by allowing his eyes to wander around the room.

It was surely a chore, to relax with her.

He sips his drink through a tiny red straw. The bar fills up, and he makes eye contact with the young man, who has just bellied up to the bar stool next to him. The young man is wearing a *Bush/Cheney* button on his shirt. He already has the same 47-year-old gut, that Mr. Exciting Guy has allowed his body to do to him.

Also, the young man has less hair than Mr. Exciting.

He introduces himself as CJ and asks Mr. Exciting Guy about Star Wars. He's giddy and thrilled, to have just purchased a new improved *DVD* collection of the first three films. Mr. Exciting Guy does not have fond memories about the series. He thinks they should have been called *Return of the Muppets.*

Mr. Exciting Guy nods nice to CJ and hopes he's not gonna tell him anything about Darth Vader. He does appreciate that someone is giving him the time of day, at least, they weren't talking politics.

The conversation turns to politics. Mr. Exciting Guy tells CJ he's just moved, and hasn't registered in time, so he is in effect, like a felon, and cannot vote.

CJ buys him a drink.

After his fourth drink, Mr. Exciting slips off his stool.

Offers CJ his hand as an insincere farewell.

And waddles for the door.

He sees his car, gets in, stares at the windshield and into the rearview mirror. He rolls down the driver window, and lights up a smoke. He takes his cellphone out of his pocket and looks at her name on the scroll list of names. Should he give her one last chance? Will she scold him for his drunkenness, or open her arms, hold him tight, and tell him she loves him forever? He has no idea. He's Mr. Exciting Guy. But he's weak and drunk, and getting a bit less exciting all of the time.

He drives to her house. The former crazy, attractive girlfriend's car is parked in her driveway. There are some lights on. He looks at the house and then, at his phone. How easy it would be to enter the world he used to live in. He puts the seat down, ponders, and falls asleep again.

He wakes up to the former crazy, attractive girlfriend knocking on his window with a rake handle. She's screaming profanities and something about, "Get the hell out of here." He feels as if he's woken up to his earlier dream.

He starts the car, and drives off. He drives around the block.

She must have gone back in the house.

He looks at his socks that she never rolled up.

He grabs six rolled up pairs, gets out the car, and throws them at her front door.

He then drives off, back to the apartment.

No Browsing

Here I am at the Paris' house, Southside Chicago. Pinned down on the bed of Mr. and Mrs. Paris—whom I've never met—by my best friend, Patrick Flynn and, my brand-new friend, Terry Paris.

Kathleen Paris, eighth-grade sister of Terry, has an electric hair clipper in her hand. It's alive with plugged-in-current, and getting ever so close to my eyebrows. According to them, I've lost some kind of bet. And this is my debt to the, *Parents Not At Home Society* of three.

The loss of an eyebrow.

I can probably squirm away from Patrick and Terry. But the older sister is pretty, and the growling clipper, cradled in her hand, *can't possibly be the end of the world.*

Can it?

It might be best, to lose the eyebrow, as if it's just a temporary failure. I can return to this war another day.

I crush my eyes shut. I cry out. I give in, to the hair clippers wishes.

It doesn't hurt

Not that big a deal.

I am released by my friends.

We all study my newfound deformity, in the huge mirror, across from the Paris parent's now rumpled bed.

I know, that if I ever bring friends into my Mom and Dad's bedroom, with a plan to shave off eyebrows, I will get caught. My sister, Diane, specializes in tattling; she gets a lot of joy, watching her twin Dave, or me get hollered at by Dad.

Diane is learning how to play the organ, for weekend mass at St. Ethelreda.

David and I take turns hiding the church bulletin from Dad, so he isn't aware of when *altar boy training* is held.

My Dad's anger can shoot out of his mouth at any moment, like the tiny tools from his *Swiss Army Knife,* which I'd left in the rain. Dad rarely spanks, but his red words rattle me, into a boy with a Jell-O spine. I can't be understood, by even myself, if I choose to speak.

It's best in my house, to blame all gloom and doom on my older brother, Dave.

Everyone assumes he did it anyway.

This is best for my survival.

~ ~ ~ ~ ~ ~ ~ ~ ~ ~ ~ ~ ~ ~ ~

There's this new kid at school. It's the right thing to befriend him. Find out what he's like. See if he has cooler toys at his house, than Patrick or I do. Sister Vivian tells everyone in class, "Be good to the new boy."

We are good boys.

So, after school, Patrick and I walk out of St. Ethelreda's Elementary School, and catch up with Terry.

Terry plucks off his clip-on tie, rolls it up, and sticks it in his front pants, pocket. He makes some joke about, *how a girl will be happy to see him.* I laugh. I don't know any girls who would like to see rolled up clip-on ties.

I don't get it.

I look at Patrick to see if he laughs.

Patrick has a gob of booger, hanging from his nose.

112

We stop by *Chuck's Deli* where I like to buy nickel pop, and penny candy. Chuck, with dried up cow blood, on his apron, is all smiles at the cash register.

When we get outside, Terry shows Patrick and I, how he's stolen a bag of hard candy. "Come on over to my house. My Mom won't be home until 6 o'clock. It's just me and my sister at home," says Terry.

Patrick and I now have our mouths filled, with a mix of malted milk balls, and hard candy that tastes like root beer. I'm *nervous* about eating Terry's stolen candy, but I'm getting more comfortable with it. We're eating the evidence.

Terry's house sounds like an adventure. Every time we go to Patrick's house, his Mom talks so fast, in her Irish way I don't get most of what she says. I don't understand how Patrick can, but he does.

Mrs. Flynn has this way of sounding pissed off, even when she's trying to be nice.

My Mom is always home. Adventures at my house, are always *watched over* adventures. Mom's oversight keeps us from having our eyebrows trimmed, though. If by chance my Mom is not home, my brother enjoys punching me in the shoulder. So, the idea of going to Terry's house is picking up steam.

I follow Terry into his house and Patrick follows me.

"That's my sister, Kathleen," says Terry, and points to a cute older girl, who is talking on the phone, while she creates snakelike images with the phone cord. Kathleen looks like that girl on *That Girl*, and waves at us like we're nobodies. I guess fourth graders are nobodies, to eighth graders.

"Where's your bathroom?" I politely ask Terry.

"Down the hall. You can't miss it," he says.

Once in the bathroom, I feel comfortable. There's reading material. I open a Montgomery Ward's catalog and turn to *Ladies in their Underwear.* I wonder where they find people who allow pictures to be taken in their underwear. There are men in underwear, too, but I focus on a lady who smiles while she points to her pointy bra. I realize that even though I'm done pooping, I sit and continue to study the catalog. If only Sister Vivian would give us a quiz on this, I'd be okay. Finally, I use the last two pieces of toilet paper.

"Terry," I call.

"In here," he says, and I walk into his parent's bedroom. Terry has pinned Patrick down on his parent's bed, and Kathleen is cutting off his eyebrows, with an electric hair clipper. It's the same kind of clipper my Dad uses to buzz cut my brother's and my hair. Dad makes sure we start the summer looking dorky. I laugh a little. Terry lets him up. We stare at Patrick.

Patrick is blonde, and his eyebrows—now on the blanket—are blonde, so you can't really tell any difference. Then, Patrick puts on his dark framed glasses and Patrick is Patrick. He doesn't look very happy though. Kathleen tells us, "It's extremely rare, when a person doesn't have thin eyebrows, that their eyebrows don't grow back."

She looks at me, "How about you, Gary? I'll give you a dollar." Patrick pulls out his dollar, and waves it in front of my face.

As a good Catholic boy, I can't think of any useful reason, that Jesus, God or the Holy Ghost has ever given me two eyebrows. What's the harm in shaving one off? A dollar is a lot of money. I am ready to say okay.

There's a picture of President Kennedy on one nightstand, along with one of those giant pitchers, that people used before bathtubs were invented.

"I'll give you a dollar tomorrow," says Kathleen, "If I can cut an eyebrow now."

"No, I think I'll go."

There's a struggle. I lose. I lost my eyebrow, to two classmates, and an attractive eighth grader. After the eyebrow is gone, the other one looks horribly wrong. I look like a weirdo.

We all agree that the existing eyebrow needs to be shaved off. I offer no resistance to Kathleen.

Patrick and I are now two guys without *over the eyeball* hair. We leave Terry's house. Patrick buys us both *RC Colas*, and *Mary Jane* candies at Chucks. It's a great snack. We both forget we've lost our battles.

I'm one of those boys who is always hungry. I'm always prepared to eat. I help Mom set the table. Hamburgers bubble in grease on the stove. Mom sets the salad down, in the center of the kitchen table, and looks at me with a cup of curiosity.

"You okay, Gary? You look pale?"

"I'm just fine Mom. When will Dad be home?" I ask.

Mom takes my face in her hands. "Where are your eyebrows?" she screams.

I totally forgot my life without eyebrows. I tell Mom the entire story, except for the stolen candy part, the Montgomery Ward's catalog, and that I think Kathleen is really pretty. I guess eighth grade girls belong on pedestals, even if they use hair clippers on little boys.

Mom calls Mrs. Flynn, and asks if Patrick has had his eyebrows shaved off. I hear Mrs. Flynn scold Patrick like he's the devil's right hand. I quickly find out my Mom and Mrs. Flynn both think eyebrows are extremely important.

Mom puts make-up on my brow-less areas before I go to school.

Dad hollers at me for allowing myself to be trimmed like a Schnauzer. He suggests I take boxing lessons. My brother and sister think this is very funny. They share the tale with all their friends. I am a dork to them. I cry and taste snot.

I'm not allowed to ever, ever, *ever* go back to Terry's house for the rest of my life. I'm also not supposed to bring Terry over to my house, unless his house is on fire. I wonder if my twin siblings, would shave Terry's eyebrows off, if he did come over.

I go back to Terry's house, next day after school.

He's alone in the front room.

I bend forward like an angry rhino,

and ram into his breadbasket with my eyebrow-less head.

He falls down on the carpet and cries.

Kathleen isn't around so I never get my dollar. I go home and check our bathroom mirror to see if my eyebrows have begun to grow back.

Not yet.

You know, to this day I trim my own eyebrows.

Pockets

"If you can guess what's in my pocket, you can have it," says the man in green jeans.

"Nah, I don't wanna guess, mister," I reply.

"Come on," he urges.

We wait in line with our choice of second-hand music at the *33 1/3 Street Record Store*. He has over eight pockets in his *places-to-hide-stuff* coat.

I attract *odd people with eclectic ways* to bring about talk without, "Hello's."

Trying to size him up I can't help but gawk at his schnozzle. It's big red and unpleasant. "Which pocket mister?"

His face caves into a *scrunch of happy* that I'm swinging at his pitch. Inquisition springs wings in his head. He puts his right hand into the bottom pouch of his dingy tweed jacket. "This one my friend," he smiles.

"Is the thing something one might want? Or is it something one might find offensive?" I ask.

His left hand holds a copy of Alice Cooper's *School's Out* album. He also has a *Casper* greeting card with the *apparition* flipping the bird. Which apparently can be done when a spirit only has four fingers. He whispers, "It's a mystery!"

"It's a stumper." I agree. "Let me put on my thinking cap."

"Think and… and… guess!"

The cash register sings its tale of retail snappiness. Everyone is giving their ear to Willie Nelson's recording about a *confession of a lie to a ghost* via an innocent ballad. The front door opens. A January breeze cools my perspiration. I'm now fourth in line to make my purchase.

I prefer my waiting time to be in a malaise of *putz*. I hold a Nat King Cole CD that I plan to snail-mail to my old man, for his 73rd opportunity to extinguish tiny fires.

I want the freedom to be rid of any anxiety about pockets.

"How many guesses do I get?"

"One!" His tone has lost its glee.

"You have a white mouse in your pocket."

The stranger looks at my face with interest. He pulls a brown mouse out of the pocket! It stands up proudly on his palm. He starts to hand it to me.

I back away, "It's not white and my pockets aren't designed for the residential placement of rodents. Plus, plus I don't want your mouse!"

"OK, OK, OK." The man puts the mouse into a different hole in his jacket. He pulls out a piece of paper, "You've been served!" He shoves my chest. Leaves *Alice* and *Casper* on the counter and pushes through the glass door with bold getaway steps.

I unwrap the possibility of a *habeas corpus* being incorporated into my humdrum machinery. The paper smells like tiny pet poop. I unfold it. It's a subpoena! I am witness for a hearing in three days in *Courtroom J* of the *Potter County Courthouse*. It is in regards, to the death of a *Christian McGee*. I have no frickin idea who that is.

I buy the Cole CD. Open the door and wish it wasn't so damn cold.

I sit in the theater of justice earlier than the prescribed time. I stand for the Judge. Plunk my butt down at "his honor" and watch people's lives get expunged validated divorced lectured to and "continued" into convenient times for the attorneys. In this handsome room with knotty wood the judge calls a recess. I think of grade school.

Someone left a newspaper. I flip it about and find my horoscope for yesterday. The obits are on the same page. There's a tiny picture the size of a *Forever Stamp* of the stranger who served me the foul-smelling subpoena at the record store. It's Christian McGee *now deceased!*

He was 49 years old. Beloved husband of Rebecca. Beloved father of thirteen children, all with first names beginning with the letter *P*. A member of *St. Barbara's Parish* blah blah blah. In lieu of flowers donate to the small animal department of the *Potter County Humane Society.*

An image of *Pocket-Man* flashes in my mind. I'm spooked. A parade of children—with names like Pascal Perry and Patricia—plow through the courtroom doors. Shivering I shoot to my feet and dash out with the crumbled subpoena in my fingers.

Rambling

Every April 16th, my landlord is happy because his taxes are done, so he knocks on my door holding a screwdriver. He wants to know if it's ok to tighten up the screws in my basement—I mean garden apartment. I say, "Ok," and wish I was watching something nobler on TV.

But I'm not.

He tightens loose screws all over the place. Mostly on light switches. Then he goes upstairs, and bothers Maude. Maude reads tarot card fortunes, for people who want their future told. She has three regular customers.

One time, Maude came downstairs, and asked me for a cup of sugar. All I had was Stevia, and she said, "That won't do." Her place is bigger than mine, but I have more stuff than she does.

I'm marinating a chicken breast right now.

Today, Maude is going to the store for sugar. I ask her to get me fancy mustard. She says, "The place I'm going, doesn't have mustard."

Ok, I met a woman who said to me, "I was in a circus, and rode elephants."

I said, "Wow."

Then she asked me for some of my French fries, and I said, "Yes."

Before I lived here, I lived in a house, and didn't want to pay for garbage pick-up. So, I dumped my garbage bags in a big apartment complex, where I have a friend named Robert. Sometimes Robert and I, watched his TV together. He likes doctor shows.

So now, I live in this apartment building, and all of the sudden— maybe it's my *doppelganger*—is mysteriously filling up, my huge garbage bin with *his trash*. I feel ok about it, but the landlord doesn't like it one bit.

So, he has me keep *MY* garbage can in the garage—and, wants *ME* to *pull the can to the curb* every Sunday night. I ask him if Maude and I can switch every other week, because I don't like it. He says, "I'll talk to Maude."

But I talk to Maude, and he hasn't asked her about it. So, I ask Maude, "Will you switch with me?"

"No."

So, I'm inclined to visit Robert.

Bring my trash to his place.

And watch doctor shows with him.

I don't appreciate responsibility, and I wish Robert would watch *Gunsmoke* reruns, but he doesn't like it. At least he's respectably sincere, about his mass of *medical show mania*.

So far, the garage doesn't smell like anything, because it only holds Maude's trash. I can't help but wonder, what Maude wants the sugar for? Probably a pie. I don't know if you can bake it with Stevia anyway.

I always tell strangers that I am recovering from surgery.

I get one of those looks, *stay away from me*, or a *lovely pity*.

Pity only lasts for a short time.

The world forgets about *pity* pretty quick.

I sign up for this *work at home* thing. I stuff envelopes with pornographic literature for 20 cents a stuff. The letters are written in French, so I don't know what they say.

I gave my cell phone to a homeless person, because I wasn't getting any calls, and sometimes the text ring would go off, and there wasn't a text.

The homeless guy knocked on my door.

Asked if I would pay for another month.

And he wanted my charger.

I made him a cup of tea.

So, I really should stuff more French porn literature into envelopes. I'll do it for a while until *Gunsmoke* comes on. I can't pay solid attention to *Gunsmoke* when I'm stuffing.

My neighbor has a big rip on his bath-door screen. Bugs eventually make their way inside. I really, really want to get my duct tape, and repair it. But I hold myself back. It's not always a good thing to *volunteer* help to situations. I never see the neighbor, but I see lawn chairs have been moved about.

It's bad at the public library. You can hear people on their cell phones, not talking about books.

I've thought about taking pictures of holes in screens. I assume that tears are made by children, who don't listen to their guardians.

I remember being properly shushed by the male librarian in high school, and I really didn't do nothing loud.

The guy who lives in the apartment above Maude died. He laid dead for four days, until Maude found him when she was asking for more sugar. I found him second. It was hard to tell what happened. I looked around his place and found an envelope with 34,321 bucks in it. I put it inside my underwear. It tickled. I still have the 31,433 bucks. All I know, is the guy was named Ramsey. He didn't talk to Maude, or me, but he did have plenty of sugar in his pantry.

The police came by. A guy from the funeral home named Kevin, put Ramsey in a body bag, and carried him down the stairs by himself, because some guy named Mark called in sick. Kevin was having a hard day.

I get HBO with the extra money, but I don't watch it as much as I thought I would. Robert used to have a Playboy channel, but he gave it up. He never explained the reason.

TV is costly. It's a hassle to start or stop things.

No one ever knocked on my door to ask about Ramsey. His apartment has been empty, ever since Ramsey perished.

I should have asked Kevin, "Do you want help moving Ramsey down the stairs?" But I was thinking about stuff I would do with the 31,433 bucks.

If Maude dies in her apartment, I will help Kevin. But chances are, Kevin's helper Mark, will help. This doesn't mean I want Maude to die. She's not the nicest person, but I don't wish things like death to happen to common people.

I don't miss my cell phone, and because of Ramsey's money, I don't mind paying for the homeless guy's phone calls.

One time, a homeless guy asked, "Can I use your phone to call my mommy?"

Of course, I said, "Yes."

He used harsh language to his mommy.

And then used pleasant language to thank me.

Sometimes the landlord stays upstairs in Ramsey's place. He drinks beer and listens to baseball on AM radio. He does this when his wife is mean. Husbands aren't supposed to be mean back. Husbands are supposed to mysteriously disappear for a couple of days, and then be welcomed back with open arms.

That's what happened at my house, until Dad said, "I'm running out for some bleach." And never came home.

Sometimes I get paper cuts from envelope stuffing. It's possible this is Canadian work, 'cause some Canadians eat, and speak French. It doesn't really matter what country is giving me paper cuts. They recommend I wear rubber gloves for stuffing.

I missed Dad for about 37 days, then I joined *Glee Club* at school, and I was ok.

Mom took up *line dancing* at a saloon.

And got colored streaks in her hair.

She got the idea from a Walgreen's commercial.

She was happy when I moved out.

I was too.

I'm thinking of ways to spend *that money* in a non-suspicious way. *That money* is laying between my box spring, and my mattress. That mattress has had a total of seven people sleep on it, that I know of. TV and radio spots tell us, we should replace the mattress more often than once a lifetime.

I need to buy toothpaste. Why don't they call it teeth paste? At least toothbrush apparatus is less expensive than a mattress.

People worry about sleep.

I worry about other stuff.

But I don't worry about anything with a thermos of concern, warm or cold.

Mom still sleeps on the same mattress that Mom slept on with Dad. If it still works, why fix it? That's what she says about her *ashtray collection* too.

If I drink too much caffeine, I get jittery and feel like walking into a *not prickly bush* to stabilize myself. My doctor suggests I *not drink coffee* and don't walk around *Southern Arizona* where there are lots of cacti.

My brother-in-law said, "The first time I saw your sister; I knew I was going to marry her."

I see a woman two times a week and, say to myself, *that's the woman I want to marry.* Then, I decide marriage is awfully complicated. I'd probably have drastic changes on my taxes, and what if she wants to share my toothbrush? And I let the women go, because she was never between my fingers anyway.

Love is a *splitting migraine,* like the song that's never been written goes. Sometimes, I carry a book I have no intention of reading around with me, so I look like I have an intelligence, beyond being a regular guy who watches Jeopardy. Today I am carrying a *Roget College Thesaurus.* The word thesaurus sounds like a wise dinosaur. No one really knows anything for positive sure.

Sometimes I hear what Maude is watching on TV. She revs up the volume on the 4th of July, and stomps along to *Sousa* marches. I have cracks in the ceiling.

I told a priest about the money I found in Ramsey's apartment, when I was in confession. But I wore a hoodie, mom's sunglasses, and a button that said, *I voted* as a disguise.

I lied.

I told him it was $112 dollars. I was kind of forgiven. He told me to say 14 Hail Mary's. When I was done talking about my sins, and the bad weather coming, I couldn't remember all the words to the Hail Mary. I still have 13 ½ Hail Mary's to go. It's been a few months, but I'm on my journey to forgiveness.

Robert can help me get the right words.

How come nobody ever made *Hail Mary* into a song?

Then I could remember it.

It, the prayer is a unique football play.

Roadshow

It's a nasty thing WLS radio is doing to my ears in 1978. It can easily be heard at night via AM, through the undistinguished plains, between Chicago and Normal, Illinois.

A three-minute song suggests *joy* can be had at the YMCA.

Leisure suits might glide across disco-balled dance floors glorifying Gloria.

Rod Stewart is the worst.

He trades *rock and roll* for the question, "Do you think I'm sexy?"

My brother and I, though apart 132 miles from our parents' suburban home, and Illinois State University, still hold a pledge for the darker sounds of the Doors, Deep Purple, Stones and Black Sabbath. It's still a thrill to take a walk on the *Wild Side*. It's an agreement to spit when the *Bee Gees* rule the airwaves.

We hold this brotherly bond about music.

Talking about *the potholes of our life* trips doesn't translate.

We can always share *Marlboros*.

I broke up with Georgine Harold at school. I made the mistake of falling in love with the prettiest girl in my Shakespeare class. Then she came home from a home visit with her parents with an engagement ring.

She said she was sorry.

I need to make a massive change in my life.

I change my major from English to Sociology. Sociology sounds like something. I'm failing at grammar class anyway. I really want to drive a truck or bartend after graduation. I was never on a road to make my folks proud of me. I don't think the study of group behavior has a brotherhood with semicolons or apostrophes. It will be a welcome change.

One day the phone rings at my residence: 800 Apple Street. My housemate hands me the phone. It's my brother Dave.

"Would you like to drive out to New Mexico and visit Diane over Spring Break?"

"Yes" I say without thinking.

"I'll pick you up Friday at two-o-clock."

"Cool" I say.

My sister Diane is Dave's twin. She's doing a nursing internship on an Indian reservation in Taos. She suggests to Dave that we visit. Dave will rescue me from a depressing reel of *noir film* running non-stop in my head after my break-up. The movie stars Georgine Harold as the villain. I know it's a big deal for Dave to take a week off work from the *produce department* of Jewel. It's like my voyage has turned from something bitter into an ounce of possibility.

I may look forward to something again.

I hear a beep. Dave pulls up the driveway in his mustard colored *66 Mustang*. I hear the stereo; Ray Davies and his kinky cronies singing about a girl whose name rhymes with cola. I note Dave has a new girlfriend in the front seat. Her name is Sue.

I had looked forward to Dave. I looked forward to hours of *rock* on the 8-track player. I quickly learned I'm relegated to the back seat. Sue is beautiful, too beautiful to sit in the back seat. I am not feeling beautiful.

I climb in the 2-door sedan into the back seat. I sit next to my paper bag filled with socks, underwear and T-shirts. The rear speakers drown out some of their banter. Dave and Sue aren't interested in my college existence or my recent break-up. They have no questions. Sue's hand is on Dave's hand which holds the handle to the transmission.

There is no place to hold a drink except between my knees. I love this car. Rather I love driving this car. I already know I hate the backseat. I nod off.

I wake. We're still in Illinois. We find out our state's rest stops don't have bathrooms. Only grass and redwood picnic tables. Dave and Sue aren't holding hands anymore.

"What did I say?" Dave asks her.

"Nothing," says Sue.

I can't think of anything to add to their sparkling conversation. I feel as a brother to Dave my remarks might sound like something he might say. I might say the wrong thing. So, I sit in silence listening to Deep Purple. I imagine smoke coming out of Sue's ears. I stare out the window looking at our state's phenomenal plains of boredom.

After a bathroom break at a Shell station, I arm myself with 4 Clark bars, and a Dr. Pepper. Dave must have remembered whatever dreadful thing he said to Sue they are kissing while gas pumps into the gas tank.

They are making up.

In Missouri Sue tells Dave, "You slurp your coffee too loud."

I don't think slurping can be a roadblock to a successful relationship.

But I am wrong.

Dave can't promise not to slurp.

For God sakes he used to work at 7eleven. Part of his job was pushing Slurpee on the public. I don't know it's possible, but I sink even lower in the back seat. She will certainly learn more of Dave's disturbing habits as their loving relationship continues to bloom. He's always for *developing gross new habits*.

Sue does something that makes me even sadder. She shoves an *ABBA 8-track* into the player. She sings *Take a chance on Me.* The tape runs at least three times. I want an excuse to leap out of the car and hitchhike the rest of the way. I'm pretty sure any stranger who picks me up won't expose me to *Swedish pop.*

It's Texas when Dave lets me drive. Sue sits in the backseat next to my brown bag of dirty clothes. She's not happy. *The Doors* rattle the speakers, *L.A. Woman.*

It gives me hope.

Then the 8-track player eats up the tape.

I miss Jim Morrison and his desperate summations of a desert depression.

Dave finds a station on the radio.

We listen to *Tradio*. People with thick Texas accents trade handguns for chicken wire. We stop at another Shell station. I stop at Shell because Shell sent me one of their credit cards. I don't know why they thought an unemployed college student could pay his bills but that's what the Shell folks think.

Texas never ends. Sue drives for a while. Dave discovers he shouldn't criticize Sue's driving. She tells him he doesn't take their relationship seriously. I guess because he wants her to drive faster. Dave says he does take their relationship seriously. He will try and do better. Sue tells him that he tells *little white lies.*

I'm trying to distinguish *white lies* from *venial sins*. It's getting too hard for me to follow. They're arguing. Some preacher on the radio is telling us we're hell bound. I sit quietly in the backseat wishing I was dead.

Dave says something about Sue's mom.

Sue cries in rhythm with the radio's singer singing *Amazing Grace*.

It's right then I determine I will never have a serious relationship discussion in a car going 75 miles per hour in the event that I will never enter another relationship.

Dave turns off the radio.

I think about killing Dave because he didn't tell me Sue is coming on the trip. I think about killing Sue because it would be something to do.

The thing is I thought this trip was something to look forward to. I will never look forward to *Dave and Sue time* in future. It's turned into being witness to a *sweet and sour* soap opera. I don't know why they want to share their roadshow with me.

We get to Taos.

My sister isn't home.

We wait outside her apartment building for two hours.

I am happy to rest my ass on the Mustang's hood. Dave and Sue take a walk in anger and return holding hands. They are staring at each other's eyeballs.

Diane pulls up in a blue Volkswagen Beetle. I holler at her for not being home. I take out all my *built-up anger* on her, then apologize. If I holler at Dave, he might leave me in New Mexico.

Sue uses her Mom's credit card. She flies back to Chicago after kissing Dave at the airport. Dave and I take in the Taos sites and drive back to Chicago without an argument.

Sharing Time

Entering. I try not to enter into too many opportunities unless there is a free lunch, a free set of Stanley tools, a free set of brakes or a free chiropractic evaluation of my spine. It tends to bend in a regressive manner when I *à la mode* my blackberry pie.

I enter new flukes of non-essential necessities, while speaking with Mr. Dick Sherman about his mother's knee cartilage and how he sold a product that drove the squirrels out of Brownsville. He doesn't mention what state Brownsville is in. I just assume Arkansas – ya know *Smokin' in the Boys Room.*

You can enter illiterate harmonies at your book club.

Someone is always wanting your brain to speak and dress in the asylum of fiction.

You can open the back door of chance on your computer. You just tell everyone your MasterCard will expire and, yet it isn't dead. You can get emails from tortured cattle dwellers of angst in Nigeria. You can find out why melons are so popular in Cancun and not so cool in San Juan. You can make friends with people who attend *Mighty Ducks* hockey games on Thursday instead of staying home to watch the guy who replaced Larry King.

Or you can be me: A guy sitting in a lobby waiting to waste the next 90 minutes. The *Super 8 front desk* said no more than 90 minutes— yet she is long wrong. I will speak to her of the value of my blurred existence. Anyway, if I sit through this *Time Share* procession of monstrous motley extravagance that knocks on my brain's door I win a boat ride.

If I lose a new therapist will tell me to "Shut up and listen to your gut" again. I think I will scream "gut" next time there's too much frosting on my cupcake.

I'm still waiting.

I know there's a prize for sitting through this interview.

Someone.

Not just anyone.

Certainly not you.

Will walk out of here with a bus ticket to a boat. Where…if you show the *boat guy* or *boat girl* your proof of having sat through this rational *Time Share Hell,* will only charge you half price for their buffet…that includes red beans, and blue bread pudding. And if it's your birthday you get a ticket for a reduced priced waffle iron, at nearby K-Mart.

So the guy—everyone who *sells stuff* has to wear shiny shoes, and pants that fit—shakes my hand. His gut is probably taking *Tums* when he sees the holes in my college t-shirt. He is supposed to be training the new guy Tom.

I shake the hand of Tom.

Charles, the role model begins modeling the role that no one ever wants in their lifetime, that of a *Time Share Salesman.*

Tom asks me questions about my annual income. I would have more annual income if I won more stuff or if someone famous made a big mistake and sent me a check. I am coming to realize that scratch-off lottery tickets aren't good for my mother's mental health. Although we scratch them off together, we don't feel any closer with *happy indentured servant* results.

When the Time Share man Charles asks, "What exotic places would a Time Share residence costing say, *ninety-three grand* be like?" I think of the grandiose colors, and nauseous smells of Peoria.

It isn't on his list.

He then speaks of the bad karma of vacationers, who brew coffee in hotel bathrooms.

I can't get my hands around that. A carafe doesn't have a soul, and it won't care if it competes with a raggedy Reader's Digest from 1977 for my bathroom attention. The salesman is speaking the language of people who earn slightly more than $7.47 an hour filling Goodwill shelves with abandoned figurines of wide-eyed boys who fish with cane poles. He doesn't understand that selling only the right shoe would be cool for a one-legged carnivore.

I pretend I am a proper representative of a higher-class struggle. He and Tom can probably beat me up with more than sales jargon and indifferent tie tacks. I muzzle my ability to arm wrestle with the superfluous beauty of their slang.

I give up.

I am awarded handshakes 'cause I agree to *Buy, Buy, Buy*. A happy bell rings. I pretend to be someone else in a holey shirt and unfashionable pants. Like Howard Hughes pretended he was Batman in a Nevada desert.

I sign a form.

I sign another form, and another, and another.

My prize is going to be better than the reason I came into this sales experience. Perhaps I will be able to swim with sharks and dolphins, or something like that. It's now past 90 minutes. Tom and Charles leave me alone. To allow everyone to come to realizations.

Tom comes back to the place where we spoke and signed, signed, signed.

I wasn't supposed to sign my name as Fred Flintstone, or Howard Hughes.

Charles is angry. Tom is learning there might be people like me. I'm asked to leave. A *nice* lady with a nasty smirk, hands me an envelope with a prize. I ask if I can use their restroom, and am granted that. I rinse off my face and head for the boat?

Signs of Desperation and Hope

Originally the game plan was to get a lime, salsa and chips, a case of Corona and maybe watch a video. Finally got that copy of *Johnny Got His Gun* that I've been meaning to see. I can join the antiwar bandwagon again. I've been in a rerun mode of life, listening to Dylan, the Stones and The J. Geils Band. Listening to vinyl. Maybe I'm trying to erase the gray, ease into what's easy.

It's so easy to live life alone, stoned and apathetically broke.

Days of eating Kraft macaroni and cheese, liver and instant coffee.

I lean over to put on these Goddamn shoes. I don't like the *gorge of gut* I gotta lean over. Double knots 'cause the laces are so long. I hate that. Puff goes the Camel Lights smoke thru my nose and mouth. That scratchy feeling reappears in my esophagus causing me to cough and find some pain in the chest with more than occasional moments.

My hand grabs the doorknob. My mind shifts to what's really important. Damn, I gotta get a new remote control. I wonder if Radio Shack is open. I know this teenager who has a remote on his watch. I really envy that.

I am so happy it's a sunny day.

The grass I am walking over is too long. The lawn is calling out for Lawnboy. Well, it's gonna hafta wait, 'cause I don't feel like cutting grass right now. What is weird, is that sometimes I don't mind at all.

I'm a skilled mower.

I just dread pulling that cord.

I don't appreciate it when it don't start on the first pull.

How rude of that self-propelled, green mulching bastard!

My lawn mower is a Cadillac of lawn mowers. My car is a Kmart variety Mazda 323 with weathered paint, rusty holes and a bb gun-holed windshield. But the *s.o.b.* starts me up and moves me where I need to go. It shuffles me to work and to stores. And the damn thing leaves oil like a slob. Oil stains in parking lots. I like to think of my car as a box that moves. It does not do much else.

I'm driving through downtown. My neck leans and hurts a bit when I stretch to see what movie is playing at the *Ivanhoe Theater* this Saturday. All I can tell is it's some cartoon movie. I can't believe I once loved cartoons as a kid. Now I think they're stupid and trivial. Even *Clutch Cargo* and *Speed Racer*.

I drive the mutty car past the Carnival Liquor Store and Tavern.

Do they have chips and lemon?

Why does a tavern or liquor store name itself something so jovial? Carnival?

It brings up memories of fun and…oh yeah, vomiting!

I guess it does fit pretty good for a place that serves and sells alcohol. I've never been in the tavern part, but I have bought some Red, White and Blue beer here, and I'm counting on them having Mexican beer. Just not so sure about them having chips and salsa.

In front of the store, some big dude is lying on the sidewalk, like he's dead. I drive past wondering if I should stop and help him. By golly, I am gonna turn around, and help this fellow man. It doesn't look like anyone else gives a damn that he's on the sidewalk.

By the time I turn around, and park in front of this man, there are some other people. An obese cop is pulling on rubber gloves. Another man sitting on the ground is saying, "The dude is O.K."

The man on the ground is a huge guy with a beard. All around his mouth, nose, neck, and collar of his shirt is thick real blood. He has a puddle of the red stuff next to him on the sidewalk. Enough blood to donate.

He is the size of Otis Campbell from Mayberry RFD. But he is young. He has on a T-shirt advertising the fact that he is a fan of dead racer Earnhardt. I hear the ambulance coming—that siren noise. The guy is definitely not O.K. The other guy sitting next to him—who acts like his friend—keeps saying, "He'll be O.K."

I ask if he is… *(trying to be diplomatic here)* intoxicated.

The man who sits on the ground with a Cubs hat on—which right away tells me he is a hopeless person—says, "Yeah, I think he's drunk. He fell and broke his nose." He says he heard a *beautiful thud*. The cop applies a wet towel which appears to comfort the bloodied man.

The cop asks for another towel.

Another stranger runs into a nearby store to get one.

Blood bubbles spill out of the injured man's nose.

Probably a chemical reaction between *Everclear* and the human spirit. The cop asks the Cub fan, "Who is this guy?" Mr. Cub does not know his name, but he seems sure that if we all go away and allow the man to bleed on the sidewalk, he will be O.K. soon.

Mr. Cub does not want the man to be interfered with much.

An ambulance finally arrives at the same time as the second clean wet towel comes. Young Otis Campbell is loaded on a stretcher. There are people trying to sound like VIP's talking on ambulance radios. All that's left is blood on the sidewalk and Mr. Cub smoking an *Old Gold* cigarette with a brown bag full of malt liquor in cans…and me. I'm starting to think that maybe drinking isn't all that glamorous and I should really quit!

Nahh.

What good did I do? By the time I pulled up in my car, the man had all the help he was gonna get. He'll probably waken in a rage at the emergency room when some non-suspecting medical professional tries to put a tube down his nose. Otis may pick up the medical technician by the throat and throw him into next week.

Or maybe the ambulance takes poor souls like young Otis to Potter's field where they just bury the drunk and indigent alive and eliminate all of that life-saving crap. I don't know.

I hope they don't do that shit.

I really did not do a damn thing for Otis.

I was no better than a gawker.

But, if somebody had asked, I would have helped. I would have done something.

Now I pull a wrinkly cigarette out of my front jean pocket. I take my time straightening it out, and molding it into the tower it used to be. On this sunny day, I walk away from Mr. Cub and enjoy my smoke.

I do.

This cigarette could be Cuban tobacco. It is the right thing to do at the right time.

Time for a deep thought.

Was it prophetic that Otis had that Earnhardt T-shirt on? I think not. 'Cause then, when I wear my Doors T-shirt, it would mean I'm a goner. I look down at a fading, cottony Jim Morrison staring out at the world from between my nipples.

I walk into Carnival Liquor and Tavern. I use the restroom. It's disgusting. Even so, I sprinkle a handful of *well-water* on my face. It feels better; even though I'm in the disgusting little room. Someone has carved,

Fuck the World into the door with a crude object. I think it's a weird thing to be so universally profane.

I leave that john.

I find my lime, salsa and chips. The air conditioning really feels good. It's an *unexpected surprise* to find all of these items in one place. The cashier splits her time between putting little paper price tags on Snicker bars and running back to the register. She wears an oversized sweatshirt with a caricature of Truman Capote on it. It's so baggy, I can't tell anything about her breast size—which should not trouble me—but it does to some extent, 'cause I am a male, a pig and an imperfect human.

I am somewhat mystified to find that she does not have Corona. I cannot remember if Capote is dead or alive. She puts my purchases in a little brown bag and tells me, "They might have some Corona in the tavern." What a nice smile she gives me.

I walk down the hallway to the door of the Carnival Tavern. There's a sticker with a picture of Andy Kaufmann on the door. It's always a good feeling to walk into a tavern, one of the few places that don't discriminate against you if you look and act like a drunk smoke non-stop and say just about anything that's on your mind, 'cause you're drinking. Plus, there's always a TV, and TV has always been a blessed friend of people like me, who can lose themselves for twenty-two minutes and change, on Gilligan's Island.

I sit at the bar and stare at the fanny of the bartender who looks good in those jeans. She turns around. She's wearing a shirt that celebrates the dope smoking accomplishments of Bob Marley. Bob looks pretty content smoking a *jay* on her chest. She's blonde. I ask her about Corona. She says, "I can probably come up with a six-pack, if you give me a few minutes.

"Okay." And she serves me a draft. TV is showing *Rebel Without a Cause*.

The pool table looks green and inviting. Quarters are stacked on the side and two guys are shooting stripes. The guy shooting has sweat pouring down his face. He looks uncomfortable holding a cue. There's a picture of a naked Asian woman on a mountain bike on the wall. It's perfect for this room.

The jukebox keeps playing *American Pie*. I put a couple quarters on the pool table, and one in the juke box to hear something by Patsy Cline. But the machine is determined to *Don McLean* us to death. So anyway, the guy shooting stripes finally loses. He looks at me as he walks away with a real blank, hopeless and forlorn shit-face.

The bartender still doesn't come up with the Corona.

I kneel down to put in my quarters, and notice this little strip of paper taped to the side of the table. It says, "Play until you win, then go to hell."

The balls make an abrupt sound as they fall to the rear of the table where I have to rack. I look up at the guy I am playing against. He does not scare me. He seems to limp and wears a T-shirt with a shirt over it that's not buttoned. He does not appear to have a dead guy on his shirt, but for all I know, Dean Martin, Frank Sinatra and Sammy Davis, Jr. could be lurking on his boxer shorts.

I hear another ambulance sound.

I ask this other player about the *play until you win* deal. He ignores the question and asks instead, "Do you want to bet some serious cash on this game?"

"No. I don't have any serious money." I say, "Singles and change is what I have, and that ain't gonna seriously affect nobody in my view."

I rack.

He breaks.

I pick a cue, and put the blue chalk on the tippy thing.

He starts shooting and winning. The bartender comes up to me with five loose bottles of Corona jingling in a sack. I hear *Chevy on the Levee* blasting on the cheap juke box. My chest tightens. I tell the dude, "I gotta go."

He says, "Go to hell."

I walk out and notice James Dean on the bar TV. He's arguing with the actor playing his father. I creep out without shooting a shot. I have two brown bags. I must admit that this day has been a bad day. I dream of my chair, my TV and the antiwar movie.

It's hot when I get outside, and I remember how good air conditioning feels. I sit in my car which I am always glad I do not lock.

Mr. Cub is gone.

No siren noises.

I turn the ignition and drive this box back to my house.

I can't believe it, but I find my hands are lighting me up another smoke, even after that chest pain in the bar. Instinctual smoking. I pull into my driveway and carry my stuff under my arms and my smoke in my mouth.

I hear noise in the house. It's my housekeeper, Juanita, wearing a Tupac T-shirt, and a Milwaukee Brewers baseball cap. Signs of desperation and hope. Later that night I take off my Doors shirt and put on a Buddy Guy shirt. Now, I just gots to live right.

A Souvenir

Gemma sat across the booth from me at the Junction Diner. We were supposed to meet in order to disconnect. The saltshaker needed a refill. The pepper looked alright.

She wore lipstick. Her red lips printed a memory on the edge of the coffee mug. Someone played the B-side of *Dear Prudence* a Beatles song on the jukebox. Gemma called me by my name just in case I might forget who I was. We used to come here when we had *couple* status. We talked about how bright the moon was every night. We yapped about things like drapes and carpeting or the sanctity of home ownership. Now we were supposed to talk about the end. I was supposed to pick up my things.

I didn't really care about my things 'cause all my things at her place were probably worth three and a half dollars at a garage sale.

I looked down at my coffee cup. The waitress with a nametag came over every so often and warmed up our coffee. Gemma didn't talk much. She reread a very acquainted menu like it held literary value. It was my idea to break up now. I didn't want to but I had done it.

She didn't want food.

I created the pain she felt on this Saturday afternoon.

Was I sorry?

I don't know.

I never gave her a reason. Was it just that a darkness threw me in a direction of not wanting her tenderness? Maybe I'm just a dick.

She got up out of the booth. She walked out. She opened up her purse outside the diner and withdrew a pack of Virginia Slims. I left six bucks on the table. I followed her outside. She had trouble lighting her cigarette. I took out my trusty Zippo and lit hers and I lit one of my Marlboros. We shared a cloud over our heads.

Her gloomy eyes seemed to sink into my fat face. She threw her cherry lit butt into the curb. She travelled on foot got into her brown car and drove away. I picked up her Virginia Slim. It still held pitiful tobacco life. I took a long drag. I noted Gemma's lipstick on it. I put it in my front pocket.

A souvenir.

Taffie

There is a purple kazoo on the coffee table. It's hiding out under the shade of a pliable plastic bonsai tree. It's an odd day. I received a mysterious package in the mail. I opened it with what one calls… trepidation. It's a Norelco waterproof nose hair trimmer. Someone had anonymously done something kind of… kind.

It would have been kinder if they included batteries.

Almost right away I go to my battery drawer and find a double A. I load up look at my mirror, and jam this electric tool up my left nostril. Tiny helpless hairs fall into the bathroom sink. Maybe, this tool will make me fit in better with the rest of America. It can be used to trim ear hairs too.

I'm glad someone wants me to be new and improved.

I put *Two and a Half Men* on DVR freeze so I can focus on my clipping task. The DVR is like putting your dinner in the freezer and experiencing it at the wrong time.

I can always experience Charlie Sheen later.

I refuse to watch that show with the new guy.

Like I refused to watch the second Darrin on *Bewitched*.

One must stand up for vital material that matters if one has the time. I haven't thrown my considerable girth behind any political candidate yet. Because that would involve consequential concentration on TV commercials.

The DVR in my hand treats TV ads like they're bird droppings. I'm truly uneducated about that darn 999 thing or any Mormon issues in the Middle East.

I used to have a squirrel who got inside. His name was Kevin. One day he was gone. Right now a couch pillow is waiting to comfort my head and make me forget about my bald spot.

I'm watching *Desperate Housewives* in private. If there's anyone, even Kevin, who gives a hoot about me I'd be bathed in embarrassment, to be seen watching a *chick* show. Some days I have a life that drones on like rust eats up my Chevette tailpipe. It's gonna be tough to find another automotive part like that. It's 10:30 p.m. Time for all people over 47 to slip into the possibilities of sleep.

I've just fallen asleep on this *Gettysburg Green* couch. I wake up with the need to eliminate my bladder. I spray into the commode and crawl into bed. I'm alone since my little dog Ethel Merman Jr. ran in front of a church bus last year.

It was full of people positive they're going to have glorious *after lives*.

I can't tell the rest of the Ethel Merman Jr. story. Even in my inner sanctum of lubrication I always teardrop up. Suffice to say, Ethel didn't make it to the bus's catalytic converter. Not being all that religious, I have no idea if there's a dog heaven, or a hell, or a purgatory or a limbo.

I hear some guy on the 700 club, say, "Jesus had brothers and sisters."

I can't picture Jesus as my older brother.

It would be difficult to be as *good* as he probably was.

I can't see myself wearing his old hand me downs, to *show and tell*. He seems like a dude who was tough on his duds.

I don't know if Jesus had a dog either.

Rap!

There's a sharp rap on my front door. Maybe a homeless person has bumped his head. Maybe someone has come to be judgmental about me watching *Desperate Housewives*. I switch channels to a rerun of *My Three Sons*. I think Ernie Douglas grew up to become Speaker Gingrich.

I look out my peephole.

Four people stand on my cement stoop.

I have a sixth or seventh sense, they need my help. Sometimes, when I've helped in the past, I wasn't helped back. I feel like a completely squashed dog named Ethel Merman Jr. on Edward Derby Avenue.

And to make that feeling worse...

Forget it...

I open the door.

A man in a black suit, tells me, "I'm a secret service agent." He indicates that he's on important government business. "I'm travelling with President William Howard Taft, Art Garfunkel, and Vivian Vance." A cab sits in my driveway.

Secret Service guy says, "The cabby had an ugly fight with his wife, on his iPhone, about a landfill in Pesotum. He got kinda lost. Your place looks like it might have a working toilet. President Taft needs to use a bathroom in an urgent way." Then, Secret Service guy walks through my red house, indicating that he likes my poster of Sammy Sosa. Then, he calls out, "Clear!"

Taft lifts up one foot, then the other. He really needs to go potty.

Art Garfunkel is serious in appearance even with the Larry Howard hair. Art cradles an orange Guinea pig in his arms. Vivian is in their shadow. Much like she always had been in the shadow of Lucy Ball.

"Can I use your powder room?" asks a diplomatic ex-president.

147

"Yes," I answer. And the gruff gargantuan former chief justice, walks toward me.

"Well! Where is it Buster?" He asks.

I point. He barrels forward and slams the bathroom door. I hope he doesn't have bath plans. I've heard rumors. A too skinny 60ish looking Art Garfunkel doesn't look like he can help someone get unstuck in a tub. I remember I have a little tub of generic Vaseline in my battery drawer *just in case*. Vivian Vance is much hotter looking than her Ethel Mertz character. It's strange to see her in color. She's always been a black and white person to me.

"Thanks for letting us drop by. You're very sweet" says Vivian. "You can call me Viv" she adds.

"Okay Viv," I answer.

Wise people call it a "conundrum." What do you say to someone who is, in all likelihood, dead? I decide not to bring up the defunct thing. It's easier not to think Fred McMurray is in a sitcom parenting two of his three sons in his genteel style of rearing on my 32-inch TV.

Uncle Charlie brags about how tasty his potato salad is. I'm listening for sounds of running water in a bathtub. So far, all is quiet in my bathroom. Not even an explosive grunt.

"Hey Dude," says Garfunkel. "We attended the Roger Ebert Festival. It was dry, man. We saw a documentary about a sorry Quayle in Indiana," he says.

"Sounds dry," I say. I'm trying to fit in. I want to ask him about Paul Simon. Why did Art's career suck like a filthy athletic sock when Simon won Grammy statues? But I don't ask. I wonder what his Guinea pig's name is. I don't ask. After looking up at his tall stature, I think one of his anonymous friends should send him a nose hair trimmer. He sits down at the kitchen table and plays dominoes.

I only have 17 Domino tiles left from childhood.

The Guinea pig didn't chew up anything. I let it roam on the table. He didn't shed.

The Secret Guy stands outside the bathroom door in an unrelaxed way. He probably thought he'd get assignments to protect an alive slimmer president when he signed up for this gig. Oh well. Viv scoots next to me on the couch, "Do you have anything to eat?"

I give her some strawberry rhubarb pie I bought at Aldi's, a week ago. She takes a bite and says, It's kind of dry."

It looks dry.

William Howard Taft exits the bathroom.

"I really enjoyed that book by Richard Brautigan, it makes me feel like going trout fishing."

"You can keep it if you want it," I say.

"Really?" Howard asks.

"Really" I retort. And I walk into the bathroom, and get it for him. I also flush for the executive officer. I don't think there was a lot of flushing done in 1910. Taft puts the book in a jacket pocket.

"May I use the bathroom?" asks Viv.

"Yes," I say, and she takes off toward the john.

I look at Taft, as he looks around my house.

"Should one call you Mr. President, Chief Justice, or Mr. Taft?" I ask.

"Call me Taffie," says the big man.

"OK" I answer. I like Taffie.

I don't know why, but I always assumed that after you die, you don't have to relieve yourself. But now, I think you have to.

I think this entire evening—except for the dry pie—might be a dream. I'm usually polite in my dreams, except when I'm assassinating hobbits, or church bus drivers.

The cab driver knocks, and enters my front door, "Let's go folks," he says. He looks like Ernest Borgnine, with a ponytail.

Garfunkel grabs his pig, and stands up. Taft looks at the Secret Service Guy. Viv walks out of the bathroom. She has freshened up. I want to ask her, 'How can you ever have a fondness for that mean, and stingy Fred Mertz?' She should have a wild single life like me, but, again, I stifle myself.

Viv comes to me and kisses my cheek. Then she whispers something in my ear that sounds like, "How old am I?" I just smile.

Art Garfunkel has seen enough troubled waters for one night. He looks grouchy and tired. Maybe he never said, "Goodbye" to Simon, and that's why they broke up. Who knows?

Taffie holds out his historical hand to me, and we shake. Then, he feels around in his jacket pocket, and he gives me a piece of Juicy Fruit, from 1909.

"Thank you Taffie," I say.

"Thank you, Sir. You are a great American." He says.

"You are too," I reply.

The Secret Guy whispers in my ear, "If you chew that gum, your tummy will rumple for a week."

I keep the gum as a souvenir. Maybe, I'll donate it to a museum when I'm finished marveling at it.

They pull away in a cheddar cheese, colored sedan.

150

I plop on my couch, and fall asleep with the lights on.

When I wake the next day, I write this stupid story.

The Garage Sale Thriller

I stare down at that link sausage on my white and blue plate at Merry Ann's diner. Gosh, I wish it wasn't pink in the middle. Wish my eggs were not so soggy. Wish they had sour dough bread instead of this Caucasian toast. Well, you do the best with what you have. You want to pick your battles 'cause there ain't no point in bitching about this immature sausage link with that husky Hispanic cook.

We should all be partly happy.

My wife sits across from me. A cigarette lit. She puffs the air with the fragrance of a Misty Light. A pencil rests on her ear. She leafs through a *Thrifty Nickel* newspaper. She wears a gray and pink sweatshirt she bought at a garage sale for 50 cents.

Under that, is a pink t-shirt, with a picture of a white poodle up on two feet begging—begging for something—maybe a link sausage for all I know. She bought it at the Salvation Army for 75 cents. Under the t-shirt, is a red bra, she paid full price for at K-Mart. Hard to imagine her paying full price for anything.

I'm glad she draws the line with underwear.

Her cigarette hand carefully releases the cigarette in a black cracked ashtray and her hand grabs the pencil from her ear and starts circling garage sales, yard sales, tag sales, and estate sales. She's on a crusade.

I know not to listen attentively to her yet, as she's talking to herself out loud. I hear vocalizations, "NAH, baby stuff. NAH, tools. NAH. Yuck, Silver Street. NAH."

I know I don't want Silver Street items…it's the same story of an every *weekend garage sale.* Overpriced and peppered with expensive Jesus figurines and salted with patriotic figurines.

Imagine the pressure, the horribility of having a garage sale *every week?* Well, at least their garage is attached to their house, so they can run in to fill up their coffee mug, and run inside, to pee between customers. "Are you gonna eat that sausage?" Edith asks as her fork spears my pink sausage. "No," I say, as she chews it up. She winks at me.

I smile back at her and pay the $11.67 bill at the counter with a wad of cash I made with tips from delivering pizzas all night. I leave a two-dollar tip on the table. I take a last gulp of cold coffee in my mouth. Kinda feel like spitting it back in the mug but I let it go down my esophagus and into my belly knowing I'll soon release it via my bladder.

Oh, the deep thoughts from a man such as me on a Saturday morning.

After all, I need to drive as Edith had lost her license. She just can't find the damn thing.

The Geo Metro still smells like pizzas from the night before. There's sticky little labels all over the dashboard and floor with names and addresses of folks who just had to include pepperoni and mozzarella cheese in their diets the night before. Anyway, Edith has her site on the lovely city of Savoy as a really good place to find stuff.

What is our mission?

I never know if it's to find the trumpet playing California raison figurine, to complete her set that looks so empty on our mantle without the complete brass ensemble. Is it to find Nancy Drew mysteries or biographies of serial killers like Ted Bundy or Richard Speck? Is it a mission to update our wardrobes, or to start a new valuable collection? I know Edith has been talking about Pez dispensers, so far, she only has a Gumby Pez.

On the way to Savoy, we stop at a garage sale on Els Street. This is kind of a hidden street to most, but well known to a pizza deliverer such as I, who delivered a pineapple pizza, only the night before. The tables outside the garage have valuable items; plastic spoons, glass jelly jars without lids, a plastic shower curtain never opened with an old sticker that says, "new" on it and 27 beer can huggers from the 2003 McKinney family reunion.

I look through a box of books. Edith walks back from the garage with a Salvador Dali print. The proprietor is a 50ish looking man with a Harley t-shirt under a black and blue robe. With his long hair and beard, he looks like Jesus a little. Edith has bargained him down from $1.00 to 50 cents for the print.

Most of the books in the box are written by the wonderful people who gave us Watergate. There are pictures of Liddy, and Colson and Dean on separate jackets with lovely grins. Edith is so proud of herself with the print. She talks about getting it framed. I kinda know she never will as she never framed the print of the dogs who played cards for me as she has promised so many times. We wave goodbye to Jesus as we drive away.

We stop at a Jimmy John's sandwich shop and Edith runs in. She buys two loaves of day-old bread for 25 cents each. Thank the good Lord for quarters.

Edith has an eagle eye for spotting these sales. I have a gift for making this Geo Metro pull amazing U-turns. We are quite a couple.

It's understood between us that I'll garage sale with her but I draw the line on going to Gordyville for monster swap meets. Oh, she has girlfriends that will go to those.

We stop at another garage sale on Beaufort Street. Gosh, the cars that are parked here. It must be a gold mine. I'm hoping to find a CD, maybe some cool retro jazz. We park on the street. We hold hands as we walk down the driveway toward a garage. Their bushes need a trim. Many people are moseying back to their cars without any treasures.

It's a massive disappointment.

These people want a dollar apiece for used coffee mugs.

Used cassette tapes for 75 cents.

A hide-a-bed couch they're asking $100.

And a kid asking 50 cents for four ounces of Kool-Aid.

Edith and I encircle the tables of over-priced treasures with the same sense of gloom. These folks are asking an arm and a leg for their stuff. With a sense of doom, we drop our heads and head straight for Sunset Lane in Savoy where our cheap dreams might actualize.

Before Savoy we stop at Rich's gas station, as its regular unleaded is $2.12 a gallon. I put ten dollars in the tank. Edith goes to the restroom and returns before I'm done pumping. She looks happy in her cheap clothes. She walks with a spring in her step. She's doing what she likes. She really doesn't ask for much and when she does ask, it usually costs less than a dollar. She asks me, "Can you buy me a piece of Bazooka bubble gum?"

"Yeah, I can do that." I go in and pay for the gas and the gum.

As I drive toward Savoy she puts her hand on top of mine resting on the emergency brake, between the two seats. She chews her gum. I ask her to open up my Mountain Dew.

She does.

"Oh, there's a sign," she points.

"Okay," I point the Geo Metro toward an old house. It's on Heath Street. It's an old brick bungalow with lots of ivy swallowing the house brick by brick. A man who looks like the guy in those Medicare commercials carries a colossal pink bucket to his car. It's a helluva bucket. Edith climbs out first. I spill Mountain Dew on my crotch. It's cold. "Edith see if they have any pants in there will ya?"

"Sure Sweetie," and she walks off with a pocketful of quarters.

I try to get comfortable. In the rearview mirror a dog bobs his head behind the back seat of the Geo in time with Bob Dylan's song about *Hurricane Carter* that's playing on the tape player. I pick up the Thrifty Nickel to read. I like to see how much people sell their used cars for.

I miss Edith. 'Where is she?' She knows my crotch is suffering from carbonated green soda pop, for heaven's sake. She could at the very least come and tell me there ain't no pants for me. I'm a little mad, but a little bit sure there must be a good explanation.

I get out of the car and pull my shirt out of my pants so the little world of people at this sale won't think I peed on myself.

I walk down the driveway. It's an old brick one-car garage. The welcoming committee are houseplants of all shapes and sizes in ugly dirty pink pots. The plants are bright and very green.

The sale is cool stuff. There's a table full of outrageous lighters, ashtrays—someone must have quit smoking, think I.

I really like the *Tijuana* ashtray one of a sombrero. There are wax candles of Buddha and Teddy Roosevelt and a multicolored peace sign. Music crackles out of a cabinet-sized stereo. Upon closer inspection, I note it's playing an LP of Emerson Lake and Palmer. I almost trip over a miniature rhinoceros on the concrete floor. And on the floor, I see boxes of albums, tapes and CDs that I'd love to pour my eyes on. This is pretty cool,

There are clothes too. I see a man flipping the ELP album over being ever so careful not to get his fingerprints on the vinyl. He has a Lowe's canvas nail apron around his waist. He wears jeans and a t-shirt that says *Robert's Foods, Inc.* on it. There are other customers walking up. I stare at a Jimi Hendrix poster on the garage wall. Jimi is actually puffing out cigarette smoke.

Albeit the coolness of this sale and the cool sensation the Mountain Dew is still bothering me, I wonder, *where did Edith go?*

"Did you see my wife? She's wearing a gray sweatshirt?" I ask the man in the Lowe's belt.

"Can't say I have," he retorts.

"I dropped her off a few minutes ago."

"Well, sorry, there have been a lot of people here."

I walk back to the Metro thinking that she may have walked back. She hasn't. I jump up and down. I feel like crying. I try hard to make myself come together. A little voice inside tells me to "settle" much like Edith would tell our puppy Baxter, when he jumps up on me.

So, I'm in "settle mode." I walk back toward this garage sale combing my hair with my fingers creating a greasy look. I want to snoop, to look into this fellow's basement. It only seems logical that Edith would walk into his cellar door to look for more treasures.

The proprietor is selling a Yahtzee game and a DVD of *Midnight Cowboy* to a teenager. Part of me wants to be Mr. Moral, to inform the proprietor that he's selling an X-rated film to a kid – but I let it go. I continue to catalog this proprietor's improprieties just in case he has kidnapped my lovely Edith, and put her in his torturous basement.

I try to shake these thought from my head. I stand and look firmly interested in a copy of *Women's Wear Daily* magazine from October of 2002.

I breathe hard. I sigh. I want to jump up and down. I look back at the street, and can only see the toy dog's head bobbing. The proprietor changes a record from ELP to the soundtrack of *Saturday Night Fever*. The needle of the player rides a warp as the Bee Gees ask, "How Deep is Your Love." There's crackle in the air.

The proprietor gives me one of those, 'Are ya gonna buy anything?' Looks.

One of his neighbors or friends breaks our little stare down. The proprietor is reporting the AM brief sales history to his friend in exchange for a cup of fine coffee.

I stare at this magazine. I'm reading an article of how Roseanne Barr had lost 20 pounds in 45 days by eating a lot of peanut butter. It doesn't make sense. Nothing Roseanne did ever made much sense. I look at other magazines, too. There's a 1977 July Penthouse but, I'm kind of embarrassed to page through it with folks about. Who wants to be judged to be a pervert so early in the day?

The Bee Gees *How Deep is Your Love* song has ended, but it still echoes in my head. I know my love of Edith is deep, pretty <u>damn</u> deep. I know I love her really pretty damn deep. I put my hand in my shirt pocket and pull out a Misty Light. I light it and walk back to the Metro. In the backseat, I see her gray and pink sweatshirt. It's a sure sign she's been here. The Dali poster is on top of it

That seems really odd.

There's a big pizza sign back there as well that magnetizes to the top of my car when I deliver pizzas. I think that sign helps my reception.

I squash the Misty on the curb.

There's a skinny girl walking away from the sale with a big wiry squirrel catcher cage. I had not seen that at the sale. That proves this proprietor is a trapper.

I walk back to the garage thinking 'Edith is around here somewhere.' The proprietor looks at me suspiciously as he sips his coffee. There's a young family all dressed in jeans and tie-dyed t-shirts shopping. The kids seem fascinated with the phonograph as the needle dances over the album warps like a little car on a ramp going around and around.

I find myself walking and staring at the dirty windows of the garage.

"Can I help you?" asks the proprietor.

"I'm still looking for my wife," I reply.

I sit on the floor and look at a box of albums. I decide to buy some even though I don't really want them. I pick out *Bridge Over Troubled Waters* by Simon and Garfunkel, and the greatest selling live album of all time *Frampton Comes Alive.*

I inspect the albums for scratches and they're fine. As I pull the money out of my pocket, three pieces of Bazooka bubble gum trickle out of my pocket with my wad of cash. I pay this guy $2.00 for the music. I figure maybe I'm buying more time. "Thank you," says the proprietor.

I walk back slowly and stoop down. I squat at a basement window and pretend to tie my shoe. I peer into his basement window to see if my Edith is down there. One of the albums slips out of the cardboard sleeve and rolls toward my car. It parks on the grass. I feel like jumping up and down again.

I talk to myself, 'Settle.' I think of the dog Baxter. It makes my heart slow down.

I pick up the album, and put it in the sleeve. I notice the song *Cecilia* is on there. I remember every time my mother took me to the orthodontist when I was a teenager that *Cecilia* song would come on the radio. This thought settles me. Gosh, maybe I could call my mom.

I sit on the Metro. I light another Misty Light. My ashtray is overflowing with butts. I open my door and dump the butts on this guy's curb. I don't think he sees me. I feel sad. I really miss Edith. It isn't like her to do this. I can only imagine the proprietor is all about evil. Damn – he probably has a half dozen beautiful women in his basement. I drive around the block real slow. My eyes use all of their peripheral abilities to scout out my beautiful Edith.

It's fruitless, this mini search. She must be in his basement. I imagine her in terror, probably chained to an old bed frame, afraid she'll never be able to go 'garage saleing' with me no more. She's stuck in a basement room forever with somebody else's cellar treasures.

This tape I made is playing some Nilsson song. It's so stupid it makes me want to cry. It's about a doctor and a coconut. I want to jam one of my new LPs in the cassette deck. I want to stop driving. Christ – all I want is to hold her hand.

I stop driving. I put the pizza sign on top of my Metro, so I look like I'm supposed to be here. I walk half a block toward the sale. The tie-dye family is stuffing the giant phonograph into their Escort station wagon. I walk around the house. A basement window is cracked open. I stoop down and push the screen in. I can squeeze in there.

I do.

I go headfirst and land on a Maytag dryer.

There are some matches on the washer. I put them in my pocket. There are pennies everywhere too. I put them in my pockets too.

I walk in the dark.

I light a match.

I light the whole book.

I use it as a torch to search for Edith and any other damsels in distress for that matter. I come upon a family room, there's no one there. There's a life-sized cardboard cutout of Austin Powers, his yellow teeth glisten in the torchlight. On the wall is a framed picture of dogs playing poker. Edith had always promised me a framed one of those. I try to take it off the wall.

The lights come on and a policeman comes in the door. It's a familiar face, Officer Wood. I've seen him before, maybe delivered him a pizza.

"Hey, Eddie whatya doin?" he asks me.

"I'm looking for Edith."

"Oh, Eddie, you know Edith is in heaven. Oh, Eddie, you aren't taking your medicine."

Oh, Eddie…

I hate when he says that.

Before I know it, I'm walking up wooden stairs. I'm being escorted ever so gently into Wood's squad car. He puts his hand on my head as I enter the squad car. I feel like crying. He doesn't know that Edith was with me all morning.

This time I cry.

I sob.

I miss her.

As we pull out there seems to be a lot of people out on the street. Some neighbors. Some garage sale customers. And a brown haired, petite woman wearing a shirt with a poodle begging on it. She seems to be crying too and chewing a big wad of gum.

She throws me a kiss.

I throw one back. I notice she has a poster stuck under her arm.

The Living Room

The living room housed two people. They didn't use the bedrooms. Duane the son, always fell asleep in the Lazy Boy with a TV dinner and a Coca Cola. The reek of stale generic cigarette smoke clung to him. A TV tray stationed next to him held remotes and empty soda cans.

Momma was not really Momma anymore. She couldn't do much except accept the actions of others, mostly of Duane who managed the living room pretty well. Sure there was an uncomfortable clutter, too much trash, too much stuff. Some would say the whole living room was rubbish except for the new hospital bed Momma never left.

There was the stack of new adult diapers to put under her bottom when she had a BM. There were oxygen tanks. But Momma always pulled the tube away from her nose.

Duane, the good son that he was wasn't gonna have her hands tied to the bedrails like they did at Mercy Hospital. Duane didn't use the oxygen. The expensive-looking oxygen tanks collected dust along with her wheelchair, the top of the TV and the figurines on the knick-knack shelf. Truth was…the living room's medical equipment was creeping into the dining room.

Duane talked to her when he stole a smoke on the front porch, "I'm right here Momma." He might mix a can of Spaghetti O's in the blender and scoop the pureed tidbits into her wrinkly mouth. "Please, Momma, eat."

Duane did not work. He had spent some time in a penitentiary in Indiana. All he had was Momma. No one wanted nothing from Duane, except Momma. He made Momma's government check work for both of them. They squeaked by.

Marcia Utterback would come by from the homecare agency and give Momma a sponge bath on Wednesdays at 3 p.m. Duane used this time to run to the market or hang around the yard and keep the dog out of Marcia's hair.

Whenever Duane used the buttons on the fancy new hospital bed to get Momma to sit up, she moved her neck about, opened her eyes wide and said, "I'm hungry." Duane learned after a while that she wasn't always hungry when she said that.

If you looked deep into Momma's eyes, you could see the tiny white *Frisbees* in both her eyes, cataracts is what they were. Some days Momma rambled on about a little baby who was lost in a forest. Some days she had more wrinkles than anyone could count. Her wee face crumbled into a picture of pain. She was someone you just had to pity. Duane fed her half teaspoons of praline ice cream. Her face lost winkles on those days. Praline ice cream was something to look forward to for sure.

So it went for Duane and Momma.

It was the heart of a Saturday night. Duane changed channels. An intense pain struck his arm and rode an accelerator of torture into his chest. He couldn't change the channel no more. He couldn't get up to get an aspirin. Maybe it would pass.

He looked at Momma. She was in a nice sleep, "Momma I love you." He looked for some miracle of help from her, but she just rested. When he used his voice, it hurt. He didn't know where the cordless phone was. The TV was locked on C-Span. Dennis Kucinich, the presidential candidate talked to a crowd in Ames, Iowa, about the need for national health insurance.

A cold spirit wrapped a tightening band of death around Duane. It whipped up a cold dusty air over Momma. Duane's spirit exited out of the fireplace's open flue. A little bookend with a little boy and a pony fell off the mantle, onto the hard slabs at the foot of the fireplace. The ceramic boy broke free from the pony and now lay beside a dust bunny.

Momma just lay there. She didn't know her Duane had breathed his last whiff from the living room. She probably felt cold, especially if she had made a mess under the blanket. She just laid there at the mercy of anyone who might come by.

Momma's thoughts danced without music. Recurring memories of that baby lost in the forest, cold, and wet and helpless. Please, somebody help that child.

"I'm hungry," thoughts mixed in with the baby, the forest and the hopeful desperation. A vision of fishing with her daddy a million years ago in a little blue rowboat, worries of not being able to pay for this or that. Anxiety about being tossed out on the street.

The baby kept coming back like the chorus of a song.

A bite into a slice of cold orange.

Juice was everywhere on her chin.

Nice sensations worth a smile. She saw her toddler son through the eyehole of a camera as he sat on a pony with a cowboy grin. She danced with Lawrence Welk in a studio in Hollywood. He kissed her cheek. Visions of holding a spatula over a hot stove of lively sizzling bacon and eggs. A teapot whistled. She felt a phenomenal peace as she rested in her husband's deep thick chest.

Wind splashed her face like a wave of comfort. She stood on a riverbank watched a shooting star shim through the sky. The little boy screamed for help. Momma's eyelids reopened.

Outside the living room, life went on. Bees enjoyed her flowerbed. A neighbor's lawn mower drowned out the sound of Duane's dog scratching at the back door. A newspaper slapped the front step on Monday, Tuesday and Wednesday. A whippoorwill sang his early evening serenade. Mitt Romney was on C-Span, talking about faith.

No one really knew if it was a good spirit or an evil spirit that took
away her valuables her sight
her hearing
and her walking,
Her senses were robbed from her one by one.
Now that spirit took her baby, too.

She's in a living room where nothing mattered anymore. Her hands were full of BM and she spread it around like finger paint. She knew enough to understand if she slept again, the lost little boy would be back and no one but her ever heard his calls for help. Three days of tears in the living room.

It's Wednesday at 3:20 p.m. and Marcia Utterback is running late. Marcia is surprised the front door is unlocked. She entered the living room and saw Duane's blue, and purple face. She emitted a squelched scream. Momma was in disarray in the soaked hospital bed. Marcia ran outside and dials 911 on her cell phone.

A tearful Marcia staggered back through unearthly odors and clutter into the living room. She puts on latex gloves, and cleaned Momma. The ambulance attendants swept up Momma, onto a clean gurney and took her away from the living room forever.

The Posse

A cold rainy wind blows between these wood slats. Some nights, I stuff straw, or pieces of raggedy cloth into the slats, to protect me from the dusty, gritty rain. It's never enough. The wind blows it back in my face, with a whipped-up vengeance. It's best to give up the fight, and accept the misery of the elements.

My filthy shirt, and pants are as weathered as the slats that protect these tall horses. My boots have damages like world travelers' suitcases with labels saying where they've been. One leather scrape might be from a critter that wouldn't let go of my foot. One hole withered with old age. It grew like a wound, wider and sicklier and open to suggestions of a long painful death by disintegration.

I pull an old horse blanket over my head. Hooves shuffle around in their stalls. Horses neigh and breathe. Shit plops on the muddy floor. A rat tries to enter the comfort of my left boot. I clumsily clobber it with the right boot. The rat scatters away under a stall. Can't help but wonder why we have that damn cat! It sleeps at my feet. The rough lick of its tongue on a toe has wakened me more than once.

I've been shoveling shit in this hellhole for months now. Carmen, Montana. This town ain't got nothing for me 'cept horseshit. I'm on a list for a *hole in the wall* at Mac's Boarding House but, I gotta wait for some old fella to die before I can get a warmer place to sleep. With this weather changing to cold, maybe old John Hickey's heart will take a coughing spell seriously enough to land him six feet under. One can only wish mean-spirited thoughts when they're in a cold hell like me.

Gunfire explodes down the street. These filthy feet get even colder as I run to the window and peer out into whatever is happening down this mean road. I open the creaky door. Gunfire lights up the street like lightening bugs turning their asses off and on. I stand outside the door as some wild cowboy zig zags past me in the dark slumped over on his horse looking back at somebody shooting at him. Can't imagine him being nothing but scared. Probably poked the wrong man's wife.

With rain soaking the ground his saddle bag plops in a brand-new black puddle.

I run out. I'm a man in my fucking underwear, standing in the rain. I pick up the saddlebag and run back into the stable drenched with rain. I don't see nobody looking at me.

In the stable, I sit on a big old tree stump, and look in the bag. It's too damn dark to see anything. I feel coins and paper money inside the bag with my freezing cold hands.

There's a sharp knock on the door—the butt of a shotgun smacking wood. It's Percy Slover, the deputy, "Hey, McNabb, you awake? The bank's been robbed, and Sheriff Gates wants to form a posse." Slover is talking to me. In the dark and slop of this place he can't see I got my hand in this saddlebag. Kinda like he's talking to a shadow.

"Yeah, yeah, I'm awake. Let me get my boots on, for Christ sakes. You gotta extra gun for me? Mine is so rusty, it might fall to pieces."

"We will get ya something McNabb. Just get your ass dressed. We're gonna meet in front of the bank."

"Yeah, okay."

I take a couple coins out of that saddlebag, and look around where I might hide them. There, in the corner. I dig a hole with my hands, through mud, horseshit and broken glass. Cut my hand. Can't tell how bad, due to lack of sunlight. My own damn fault 'cause I always smash my whiskey bottles after the last gulp. Don't know why – just feels right. Put some straw over the mess, put my wretched clothes back on, and slip those holey boots on my feet.

Plum forget where I put those coins.

I saddle a big ugly horse we call Rooster, 'cause he raises hell in the mornings, for unknown reasons. Rooster's angry 'cause I woke him. He doesn't want to go outside into the rain. Find my hat fit it over my wet hair, and walk Rooster down the street.

Think about what a miserable no-thank-you job it is being in a posse.

Worse tonight than other times.

Think about them coins.

Did I put them on that tree stump I was sitting on or maybe that ledge? If my boss, Moses Zook finds them before me, he'll wonder where they came from.

Slover throws me a rifle when I walk Rooster to the bank. How am I gonna carry a rifle, and hold Rooster's reins? There's five of us who was gonna be temporarily deputized, and given the nod to kill somebody with the sheriff and God's graces.

Cheesy Williams is here. He's a short snort of a man with a big gut. He looks as bad as me tonight. Cheesy's always around to volunteer, but he can't shoot worth a damn. Just kinda like having a talkative neighbor with ya on a posse.

Butch Bond's here with his kid. Both on fine horses. Butch is the richest guy in town. Probably a lot of that money that was took was his. Butch was born with a halfway grin, and a silver spoon in his mouth. His kid is pretzel skinny and itchy to shoot a man instead of a rabbit.

I get up on Rooster, and feel the cold rain seep into my pants from the saddle. Feels like I peed on myself.

Zeke Spear rides up to join us. Zeke's a good shooter and a braggart. Always talks about how many gals he's poked. He jokes he's had more ass than the outhouse shitter. He can shoot good, though.

Sheriff Gates is an old guy. Missing teeth. He's been shot a couple times. He walks like he could use a crutch. He's a mean cuss.

"Okay, boys. Slover's gonna stay here," He says. "Some feller robbed the bank. We're gonna get the fucker and put a bullet hole through his forehead. We're gonna get the money back. My deputy thinks he might of shot the guy, but he ain't sure, 'cause it's so God damn dark."

Gates gets on his horse after two tries, and starts the parade he calls a posse. We ride off past the stable and into the cold wind that slaps my face with bitter cold rain. I sure wish I had a biscuit or some jerky to chew on—even for a moment, so I don't feel so cold, so wet, so tired, so miserable.

"Hey, Cheesy, can you slip this rifle into your scabbard?"

"Sure, McNabb." And I hand him the weapon.

At least I won't have to carry that gun. Maybe I can put a hand under my jacket to keep dry and use the other hand, switch off. I ride with Cheesy a couple of horse lengths behind Gates. Cheesy starts bitching about the cold. I just listen. "Christ, its cold out here, McNabb. I never felt so cold."

The other thing worse than the soggy chill is hearing Cheesy talk about it. Then, he tells me about his sicknesses, about not being able to shit for a week, about some monstrous boil that's buried under three inches of beard. I want to vomit myself.

"Jesus Christ, Cheesy, you should be at the doctor, not on a fucking posse." I wish he'd shut up.

We trot on, and I can't help but wonder where Gates is leading us. How in the hell is he gonna follow a trail in the rain? I wish we could stop under a tree, and *just be* for a minute. Rooster's probably wishing that, too.

"Think of the bright side, Cheesy, maybe there'll be a rainbow at dawn."

My mind flashes back to the saddlebag full of money. Maybe old McNabb will have a bit of a rainbow and a shit-faced grin spread across my face. Fine tobacco, whiskey, and a stagecoach might take me out of Montana to Reno, where a man can get a whore. Warm thoughts embrace me for a bit.

Zeke speeds up his horse's gait and has a talk with Gates. Zeke circles round. He rides up to Cheesy and me. "That sheriff don't know what he's doing, or where he's going." Says Zeke.

"Rest easy, and know you're a fine citizen helping out with this posse. Maybe if we catch this rascal, we can get a reward."

Zeke seems satisfied with that. He tells us he's never been on a posse that caught a man. Cheesy tells Zeke about his physical problems. I hurry back not wanting to hear about it again. I circle back and have a word with Butch Bond and his skinny kid, August. Then, I catch up with Zeke and Cheesy again. Zeke's doing the talking now – telling a wonderful story about him fucking a 400-pound two-dollar whore in South Dakota. Cheesy and I laugh like hyenas wondering how Zeke didn't get himself crushed.

We must have ridden for a couple of hours now. The rain's authority has been cut away to a light mist. A smidge of sun can be seen, like the sun wants to scold the clouds.

Gates turns about and we all make a circle. We're a sight for sore eyes. We was all thinking about something warm, whether it was a cup of mud, a steak or a woman.

"I lost his trail. I don't know where the fucker would go." Says Gates.

"If I was wounded, and cold and despairing, I'd shoot myself." Says Zeke.

"Don't forget he's got that money from the bank. He's probably going where he can spend it." Says Bond.

I keep quiet. I'm not minding if we shoot this bastard who robbed the bank, 'cause then he won't never come back and look for the saddlebag. Same time, I'm wishing to be in that stable trying to get some shuteye. I wasn't gonna say it out loud either, that I was lost after traveling in the dark and didn't have no idea how to get back to Carmen.

Since we're all just sitting on our horses, I slide off and step away to piss. I guess I start something, 'cause the rest of them follow suit in kind of a peeing circle.

"Dad, do you think we'll find this guy?" Says the boy to Bond.

Bond takes off his hat, looks up and watches rainwater hit his face.

"Sure, hope so, August. Hate to think we been wasting our time." Retorts Bond, loud enough for everybody to hear.

"You ain't telling me this has been a waste." Says Gates with a mean smirk.

"All I'm saying is that we haven't found the thief, and until we do, it's a waste." Says Bond.

Cheesy looks more miserable than all of us put together. He walks off to take a shit behind some brush. I'm thinking one of God's creatures would maybe bite him in the ass and give him more to bitch about. It would be hard to distinguish Cheesy's grunts from Rooster's.

"I'm thinking we should head back into town, get some grub, and head back out." Says Zeke. "In daylight we can see something. This feller's probably hiding under a rock. We won't see him in all this dark and rain."

"I'm with Zeke." Says Cheesy as he pulls his pants back up.

"We ain't gonna do no good without something in our stomachs, maybe we'll see this guy riding back to town." Says Gates.

"I'm with you Sheriff." I say, struggling to get back on my horse.

Bond starts to say something, but Gates interrupts him. "Bond, we ain't giving up. I always catch my man."

Gates looks at Bond with a squint of evil. "Good to hear." Says Bond.

Cheesy has a helluva time getting back on his horse, and as he climbs up, his hat falls in the mud. The kid jumps off his horse and retrieves it for him.

Since I was lost anyway, I let Rooster follow the pack of horses' asses and I slump forward with the hope I might sleep-ride a bit.

With the sun rising, and things lit up, four tired old bastards amble forward following the sheriff. The kid sits up straight looking right and left with pistol in hand. He is ready to shoot the bank robber. I wouldn't be too useful with that borrowed rifle in Cheesy's scabbard.

Gates rides with his head down too. What a guide. I don't give a flying fuck if we catch this varmint anyway. I just hang my head; wish I was closer to that saddlebag at the stable.

Hear pistol shots.

Lift my head.

The kid's shooting at some poor bastard who's slouched on his mare. The bastard falls off halfway. His head scrapes against the mud and rocks as his horse scampers and stops and falls on the ground.

"I got him," Says August with youthful exuberance. All of us kick our horses to look at whom the kid shot.

August smiles like he's just gotten laid for the first time.

"Good shooting, son," Says Bond.

We all trot fast to the man with the fresh bullet wound. The horse whinnies in anguish. It's been shot too. Gates takes out his gun and shoots the horse dead. We see two of God's creatures meet their maker. The cowboy is half under the dead horse.

Zeke hops off his horse first, kind of a zing to his dismount. Probably thinks this posse thing is over. He can go back to poking every female in Wyoming again, since it hasn't been done so far as he knows.

"Don't know who he is," Says Zeke, as he lifts up this poor bastard's bloody, muddy head by a handful of hair.

"See if he's got the money," Orders Gates.

"Do you see the money?" Asks Bond.

I get off of Rooster and help Zeke look in the man's pockets. The guy's pretty stiff. Zeke gets out a sharp knife and cuts some saddle straps. With the kid's help, we pull the saddle off the horse. But there's no sign of the bank's riches. Just a very dead horse, and dead cowboy.

We all just kind of stare.

"Should we bury him, Sheriff," I ask.

"No! Hell, no. Put his body on the back of the kid's horse, maybe Slover will know if he's the same guy."

The kid's glee fades into the wet sprinkle.

"Did I do good, Dad?" He asks.

"Yeah, you done really good, August. I imagine you got the right guy," Says Bond.

I help load the dead man on the kid's horse. His face is already pretty blue, lips purple. The kid shot a dead cowboy. I've seen dead men before. The kid hops on his old man's horse. We follow Gates' lead back to Carmen.

It's a sad memorial. A dead horse to mark the place that that cowboy died. A bunch of birds and critters will be having that horse for breakfast, lunch and dinner today and tomorrow. I wonder if this is the guy, too. I sure hope so. I know this feller was dead when August shot him. Hell, maybe we'll hang him dead, to kill him three times when we get back.

We was all kinda supposed to look for the loot on the ride back. The sun came out, and kinda made these cold soaking clothes a little warm. I ride between Zeke, and Bond and his kid on the way back. Kinda looking over here and there for the money.

We get to town like drowning hungry mutts. A crowd gathers round like we was some kind of heroes, 'cause we have some dead pecker sprawled across the horse.

Slover runs up, and pulls the head up on the dead cowboy, "Jeezus, this feller is real dead." Gates slowly dismounts. He stumbles as he watches Slover hold this guy's hair up. The dead cowboy has had better days.

With the mud and colors of blue, and purple stapled into his face, Slover takes a long look. "I think this is the feller," he finally says.

"Did you get the money?" Asks Slover.

"No," says Gates, and takes a brown cigar out of Slover's shirt pocket. He lights a wood match and speaks between the match's smoke,

"We'll go back out in a couple hours, and look for the money. I'll pay each of you fellers a dollar for tonight and two dollars more if we find the money."

August has lost that zest for excitement. It ain't no fun staring at a dead guy, or for that matter watching a man die. Cheesy stumbles off his horse and falls in the mud. The crowd laughs loudly. A bit of laughing does me some good, too. Maybe that'll shake things up for Cheesy. Cheesy laughs too. He has his hand on his beard like his boil is hurting.

The posse disband with the crowd. The dead cowboy, still on the horse, is being walked down the street by a teenage girl toward the undertaker's establishment. Don't think anybody else will be lifting up that morbid head by his hair to gather a look of his death.

I wake up with the sun shining eyelids of light through the slats of the stable wall. I'm so tired when I flop, I don't even check around the stable for the loose coins I left in the stable the night before. The smell of horseshit overcomes me. I slip my miserable boots back on, rub my eyes, get up and sit my ass on that stump.

I want to unbury the money and count it. I start thinking of how or when I might get the hell out of this town.

Moose Zook, my boss, walks in from the outdoors and hands me a shovel with a smirk. Moose is a large man, a moose of a man. He doesn't have a lot of horse sense.

"Why don't you earn your keep, McNabb, and shovel the shit out of here." I look up and want to say something in the ilk of *up yours*. Moose is proof of life that there is more horses' asses than there are horses. I look at Moose, and note he's wearing brand new boots. There's actually some shine on them where there wasn't mud and horseshit.

I get up and shovel manure off the ground and into a wheelbarrow. With each reach and release of shit into the pile, I get more pissed at Moose. I know that scoundrel has taken my coins and spent the money on those damn boots. Moose walks around his stable with a too-happy grin. I grit my teeth and don't say nothing but wish Moose a long painful death. I think about wiping that grin off his face with this red handled shovel, and watching him die. But I just keep shoveling. I have a bright star of a thought that I am rich. Moose only has two new boots, and this shitty stable house to his name.

Moose doesn't say nothing about finding any coins. I don't say nothing either. I hate when he stands around and watches me work. I think he knows it. I wonder if he knows I have venom in my veins wishing he'd die. I'd love to bury him in horseshit.

Percy Slover walks in tells me they was gonna go riding again, looking for that money. Percy knows I've always been one to need two bucks, so I had better go. I was almost ready to go.

"Percy, let me get some grub, and I'll be ready."

Percy puts a silver dollar for last night's posse in my shirt pocket.

"Okay, McNabb."

Moose knows the posse job is more important than shoveling shit. Even though he doesn't like it. I wheel the wheelbarrow full of shit out and dump it away from the building. I look at my dollar. I walk over to Kelley's Saloon where I'm planning on getting a meal. Cheesy and Zeke are there, chewing on pork chop bones. I order up some pork chops, too.

"Are you ready for this?" Asks Zeke.

"Yeah, I'm ready – two bucks is two bucks," I say.

177

Cheesy seems lost in thought, as he gnaws like a coyote on his bones. He looks like an animal too with that sloppy beard and mustache devouring the bone.

My plate is up. I've lost any sense of manners as I grit into my pork and slop my bread into a gravy that only tastes good 'cause it's hot.

"Damn, I'm so fucking sore since I fell off that horse," Says Cheesy. "I don't know if I'm up for this."

Zeke takes a swallow from a bottle of whiskey and hands me the bottle. I take a long drink and feel the warmth of the alcohol on the inside of my throat. I follow that with a long swallow of warm beer. I'm somewhat alert – somewhat full of grub, and somewhat baffled at why I'm joining the posse again.

We assemble again in front of the bank. August has gathered a spark of his youth back. Bond looks determined. Zeke looks like somebody who could give a damn. Cheesy is limping and hurting like a guy who got run over by a buffalo. Me? I just walk over to the stable and reload Rooster with a saddle. Moose just looks at me as I walk her out.

"Hey, McNabb, you didn't say nothing about my new boots," He says as I leave.

"They're really fine, Moose." I join the posse. I wish Rooster might buck up, and whack Moose in the face.

"Boys, we're gonna do our best and find that money," Says Gates. He's changed his clothes and his star kinda gleams in the sun.

I was thinking it might make more sense to go out by our lonesome. We'd probably cover more ground. It might be nice to ride around kinda wander lost. I could think of a plan of what I'm gonna do with that money. I know one thing I don't plan on shoveling any more horseshit no more. Can't help but wonder if some other fellers might have gone out in the meantime looking for the money.

We trot out of town. Gates has us kind of spread out in a line, to look for the money. August rides with his pistol in his holster, his eyes wide open. I guess it's about three in the afternoon. The sun does its best to dry up all these puddles. We all do our best to look at anything different in the grass and weeds trying to stretch our necks, to peer around big rocks and trees. We speed up when we see something in the grass. It usually ends up to be a dead critter.

The air feels good. I was thinking of going someplace where I can hear some guitar music. Maybe Mexico. Was thinking of buying some new boots myself, and some new clothes.

I'm looking up at the big sky a man could get lost in all them clouds. I spit on the ground.

Zeke nudges closer to Cheesy so he can open his mouth. I nudge Rooster a bit closer, too. "You know, boys, we ain't gonna find that money. I'm betting that dead cowboy hid it somewhere good," Says Zeke.

"It would be nice to find it," Says Cheesy. "But I wouldn't mind having all that money myself. I might find me that big ole whore you talked about last night, Zeke," says Cheesy.

I should keep out of the yapping about the money and what I might do with it. I might say something stupid, especially after having drank that whiskey earlier. A cold wind feels good against my dirty bearded face.

"What would you do, McNabb, if you found that money?" Asks Cheesy.

I spit on the ground. "Well, Cheesy, I'm just hoping to git a couple silver dollars for this posse ride. I'd like to drink some whiskey and get drunk."

179

"Amen, to that," Says Zeke.

The sky feels like crying 'cause rain starts pouring. The wind becomes nasty and cold again. Little sharp winds snap through me like buckshot through my shirt.

"Christ, we ain't gonna find nothing. We should go back to Carmen and get drunk," Says Cheesy.

I like Cheesy's idea of giving up. I look up and see that dead horse. We ride up on it. The rain has scared the scavengers away. The horse already has skeleton attributes. No more eyeballs, and big cavities from bites off hungry coyotes, and plucks from mean-spirited birds.

Same as last night, everyone gets off their horse and pees up their own personal storm.

"You see anything, August?" I know the boy can see well enough to kill a dead cowboy, at over 100 paces.

"No, I ain't seeing nothing," Says August.

"Gates, what do you think we should do?" Asks Bond.

"We should travel back to town slow, and keep our eyes peeled for a hint of the money," Says Gates.

It sure feels good to be off of my horse. I look at Rooster who looks like he's staring at the dead horse. I wonder what Rooster is thinking. Then I meet eyes with him. He stares dark eyes at me. If anyone knows what I've been up to, it's that horse. I'm putting him through all of this bullshit, and for all I know, Rooster has seen all of my sins.

"I wish I had a better idea," Says Bond. "But I'm betting that money is gone."

"Let's go back home and get drunk," Says Cheesy. This is his second reference to getting drunk and it sounds good to me the second time. The kid got a fat smile on his face too. He oughts to git drunk after killing a dead man. It might be a thing that some whiskey would help one to forget.

Cheesy does have some good ideas even if they're usually limited to *let's eat,* or *let's get drunk.* Cheesy struggles to get back on his horse. He's definitely not a cowboy when he mounts a horse.

We spread out and unenthusiastically glance back and forth as we ride back against the wind and against the splash of the lousy weather. I was hoping they all expected that this posse mission was a loss.

The horses have an extra step in them trots as we head back. Our not-so-heroic posse welcomes defeat with a sense of relief and an urgency to accept failure as the wind and rain seem punishment enough.

I can't help but try to hide a smile on my lips. We arrive back in town early enough for the saloon to still be open. I have this thought of giving Rooster a couple of apples as a treat for being such a good sport. It's a wonderful feeling to dismount even with the drench of stench, and rain in my boots and my raggedy clothes.

"McNabb, how about we go get a drink at Kelly's?" Says Zeke.

"Sounds good to me," Says Cheesy.

"Yeah, let me take care of Rooster. I'll meet you sons of bitches," I retort.

Bond and August take the road out of town toward their ranch. Gates struggles off his horse, ties it up and walks like a defeated old man into the jail.

Percy opens the door of the jail house. Light sprinkles on a cat wrestling with a rat. The stun of noise and light makes the cat release the rat from its jaws, and into Gates' boot. Gates is asleep on a cot, in a cell. Percy picks up the boot, dumps the rat outside, and shoves the shoulder of the sheriff, "Wake up sheriff." The cat jumps out the window to follow the vermin.

Gates' scraggy face wakes with a look of agitation. Kinda looks like them old bones need more sleep.

"McNabb here found Moose Zook dead. Somebody stabbed Zook with a Bowie knife, and took his new boots," Says Percy.

"Damn, it's a scoundrel who would steal another man's boots," Gates spits some brown stuff on the side of the spittoon.

I stand and listen to the lawmen banter. I watch old Gates stretch and fuss. The cat returns via the open window with the bloody rodent in its mouth. It hides under the cot to enjoy its prey.

I feel poorly. I'm full of rain, and crap and blood. I kind of feel like that rat, except I'm still breathing. I feel pitiful. I do not want to return to that stable.

"Sheriff, do you think I can bed down here tonight? I don't want to sleep in that stable."

"Why doncha take Zook's room at Mac's? He ain't gonna need it," Returns Gates.

I had not thought of that. But somebody died, that opened up a space at the boarding house.

"I think I will," And I leave. Percy is walking Gates to view the kill in the stable. The swinging lantern shifts shadows all over the night. They amble down the road.

I walk the different direction as the stable. I felt safer when the lawmen were closer. As I walk down the street a puppy keeps walking in front of me starved for attention. It runs ahead of me, then stops right in front of my feet. I almost trip on it four times before making it to Mac's boarding home. I push the pup away from the door to get inside.

I fumble in and Mac is sitting in a chair in the dark. He lights a wood match. "I don't have no rooms McNabb," He states firmly.

"Sheriff told me to come down and stay in Zook's room. Zook is dead," I tell him.

Mac puts out the first match in a coffee mug, then lights a candle with a second match. Tiny skeleton features on his face light up. Christ, he's skinny. He's a little rascal who has to wear little boy's clothes. His sleeves swallow up his hands and his hat droops. He's an old rusty man, in a boy's body.

"Well, if Sheriff Gates says you stay, you stay," Says Mac. "You say Zook's dead?" I can see a halfway grin on his face.

"I come back from the posse, and he gots a Bowie knife stuck up his gut. He's still at the stable lying in blood and horseshit," I return.

"Jesus, Jesus Christ, have mercy on his soul." Mac lights the third match, this time lighting a stogie that's been mashed into a dinner plate. "Gots to say though, McNabb, I won't miss that sorry son of a bitch."

I think about saying, *me too*. I thought about it earlier in the day when I wanted to wallop Moose with my shovel. I think about all the death my eyes have taken pictures within the last day. A strange thought enters my mind as I am freezing and forlorn at least that dead cowboy and Moose can rest through the rest of the winter in some kind of dark sleep.

I go upstairs and into a room. I figure it's the right room 'cause it's empty. I take off all of my clothes, and get into a bed with blankets and pillows. I feel like I'm wearing an overcoat of filth, stench and dust. I get up and see'd if I can lock the door. Not possible. I put a chair in front of the door so I can hear a noise if somebody was gonna Bowie cut my tummy. I do not have a gun. I guess I could throw my shitty boots at any intruder. I lay awake and think about the buried money, about the possibility of me getting killed. I smile as I think of what Cheesy Williams would tell me to do, *get drunk McNabb.*

I drift off when I close my eyes. I see visions of Zook with that knife in his gut. I see that dead cowboy's face being lifted up as his body hardens. I let darkness engulf me. I try not to think of Zook, but it's hard because his smell is in this bed. I want to get free of all of this. I want to get my money from underneath the horseshit and run away on Rooster's back. I do not want to end up like Moose Zook.

An image of light approaches in the crack under the door. Somber footsteps in the hall make me jumpy. My door creaks open. Cool air enters the room. A woman enters. She has a blanket over her shoulders, a dim candle in her hand. She blows out the candle, and crawls to me. She grabs my cock and squeezes it. "You want a little poke Moose? Like last night?"

I put my hands at her throat, and push her off the bed. She lands, hard on the floor.

"You ain't Moose?" She says, rubbing her sore ass.

"No, I ain't Moose."

She stands up, and lights a match and candle on the bedside table. I can now see its Lucille, a girl who works at the saloon. Lucille always follows the money in the saloon. She likes every man except for the penniless man.

"Well now cowboy, do you want a poke?"

I see her body's form in the dim light. She's round. She's grey. Damn Sam, a poke would feel good right now, maybe just what I need, to remind me that I am alive.

"I would hafta owe ya."

"That ain't gonna work cowboy," She says. "So where is Zook?"

"He's dead, I'm his hired hand"

I was thinking with my cock. I want to run out to that stable and get some money out of the dirt. I want her. How crazy to run over there and bring the money back, just for poke.

"What happened?" She asks.

"He got himself stabbed. He's dead as a doornail." I'm tired of telling folks about Zook's murder.

"He was sure living it up last night, whiskey and a lot of fun," She says with an inviting smile.

"The big ugly SOB must have pissed somebody off," I say.

Lucille wraps a blanket tight around her. She rubs her ass where she fell. I might have hurt her, but I imagine a whore like Lucille is used to getting busted about from men. She sits on a chair next to the table.

I FIND MYSELF SITTING UP IN BED, AND NOTICE MY CHEST DOESN'T FEEL COLD. "Do you know who could have killed him?" I ask her.

"I don't know cowboy, I won't miss him though, he was kind of rough, kind of like you."

"That ain't my way. I was just scared. I was wondering if whoever killed Moose might want to kill me tonight," I say.

"I wouldn't hurt ya darlin. I'm gonna see if any of these other cowboys wants a poke tonight." And she leaves the room.

I put the same dirty clothes on, and walk downstairs past a passed-out Mac. I decide to go back and get some of that money. Everything is dank. I look up and down the streets of Carmen. I feel confident I'm alone. I walk into the stable.

I feel the aura of death as I walk past Rooster. He snorts to either welcome me, or warn me of what kind of shit I might step into next. I walk back to him and pet his face. I look deep into one of his brown eyes.

I tread slow after that. I can feel the cool mud creeping into my boots. I don't trip on a body this time. Zook is gone. At least I won't have to see that bastard anymore.

I crawl into the corner where I hid the money. I sink deep in the horseshit and mud. My fingernails catch tiny pieces of broken glass from emptied whiskey bottles. I dig. Do I dig in the right place? Is the money gone? I feel empty for a minute. My heart sinks, but only for a second. I feel the saddle bag and coins. Damn, it feels good.

I put a few coins in my pockets. I want to race back to the boarding home and poke Lucille. I stop. I must think straight. There's a killer out there. There will be more whores to poke. This is as good a time as any, to saddle Rooster and get the fuck out of town. No one is gonna miss a hired hand at a stable. Lucille is probably poking another cowboy right now.

Kinda find myself back where I started. Sitting on the stump, trying to figure out what I have in the darkness of this stable. Still cold, wet, and miserable. Who killed Zook?

I make the grand decision to leave the stable, leave Lucille and leave Carmen for another town. I put the coins from the saddlebag into my pockets. I transfer the paper money into a burlap bag, and put that bag over Rooster's blanket. I put a saddle over Rooster. In my mind I promise Rooster lots of apples, but I don't want him to hear it out loud, so I'd really owe him. I walk down the stable and take whatever I want from other customers' saddles. I take a rifle scabbard from one horse stall, and a shotgun from a cabinet where Zook kept it.

I back Rooster out, and then stop and rebury the saddlebag with my boot. I hear a horse pee. I put some more of the coins in my pockets. The weight of the coins is gonna split my pants. I wonder if someone is watching. I check to see if Zook's rifle is loaded. It is.

As I ride out of town, I swear I can hear Lucille singing her fucking into the night as I imagine another filthy cowboy poking her. Still wishing it was me.

Cheesy saunters back and forth in a familiar drunken gait I've seen many times before. He lives in a little shack outside of town. I watch him struggle and I think of all his ills. I have a sneaky feeling his old haggard wife isn't gonna be happy to see him come home stumbling drunk on this rain-ass kicking night.

"Hey, Cheesy," I blurt. "You gonna make it?"

Cheesy looks up at me, "Yeah, McNabb, it's just a bit more."

I have an idea that maybe I don't have to do this thing alone. I could have Cheesy run away from everything that's Carmen, Montana, with me. He's not the best company, but he'd do anything for a glass of whiskey.

"Hey, Cheesy, can you ride a horse? I might know where that money is."

"The money from the bank?"

Rooster looks back at me with a curl of his neck, to let me know this might be a bad idea. Well, I don't know, but that's what it feels like.

"Cheesy, get on your damn horse and come with me. Might get you some of that reward money.

I don't see any point in telling him the truth until we is well on the road to leave Carmen.

Cheesy's gait gets quicker as he sputter-steps around mud puddles and gets to his horse which is tied to a post, behind his shack. "I should tell my wife."

"Nah, just come on."

I get off of Rooster and help him saddle up his horse. I wonder if Cheesy can hear the coins rattle as I get off my horse.

I help him on his horse and get a whiff of him, and his breath. He smells like a dead tortoise I had once come upon.

When he's finally settled on his ole horse, he's barely alert, probably barely alive, and he still has that lovely ambience of a rot-gut-dead tortoise about him. I look up at him, and put a gold coin in his right hand. "Let's get the hell out of here."

I struggle back on my horse and wonder what the hell I'm doing. I guess I just thought I may as well share in all of this murky misery with the most miserable man I've ever been around. Cheesy could have stayed but in all of his drunken wisdom, he chose another path to ride out with me, another nobody from Carmen, Montana.

Cheesy puts the coin into an inside pocket of his shirt. He makes belching noises as he rides with me. He is too blurry to tell me about his woes. He's drunk so for him to suggest anything would be stupid right now.

We trot south. I think it's south. Just want the whole world of horseshit, impossible posse's and the recently dead to fade away. Shit. I deserve a new start. I can't think of another soul who deserves new clothes, new boots, whiskey and a pretty whore more than me.

We haven't got more than about a half hour from town when I see what looks like a man standing by his horse. Getting some protection from the rain under a tree.

The wind pulls me in that direction. I didn't know where I was going anyway. As we get closer, I see it's Deputy Percy Slover, and he's kicking mud on something. On closer inspection, he's trying to bury up Zook's new boots.

I pull Zook's rifle out of the scabbard and ride up fast. Cheesy follows suit.

Percy pulls a pistol out of his holster belt. I hear a shot. Cheesy falls off of his horse into the mud. I somehow get off a shot with the shotgun. I hit that son of a bitch in the shoulder. Christ, his entire shoulder is gone. He's a mess of blood on the ground. "You son of a bitch, Slover. You killed Zook, didn't ya? And now, you killed Cheesy."

Slover's face has splats of blood mud, and rain and tears of shotgun pain. He looks at me, "Are you with a posse, McNabb?"

"Yeah." I lie.

"Well, I'm gonna die. I robbed the bank with that dead cowboy. I shot him when he ran off with the money. I need to ask God's forgiveness, McNabb. I need to ask God's forgiveness."

"Well, Slover, as far as God goes, I don't know but I think you are a skunk."

Slover's words become gibberish. He asks God for forgiveness over and over. He confesses to the bank robbery, to killing Zook and Cheesy, too. Blood pours a river out of what's left of his shoulder. I check on Cheesy. He looks like he's asleep, and mud and blood are blankets of his death.

I had never gotten off of Rooster. You know I felt like running over Slover with Rooster, but I was pretty satisfied that he was dead, 'cauz he stopped asking the good Lord to forgive him.

You know, I took a handful of gold coins and threw it on top of Cheesy, kinda hoping somebody might find him and bury him with a kernel of dignity. Cheesy didn't deserve for his night to end like this.

I just left the whole mess like that. Two dead men near a tree in the middle of nowhere.

I trotted south thinking about the prospect of warm feet in new boots. I felt bad for Cheesy. I wonder why he would listen to a man like me.

Trousers

You know how you sometimes look down the murky, long hallway of your flat and feel a certain defeat?

You just watched perhaps eighty-one percent of a movie about a serial killing, newspaper editor obsessed with adding ludicrous adjectives to his reporters' *Who, What, When,* and *Where,* essays.

Then, the tape breaks. The tape cartridge reacts to your Zenith VCR, like a confused man, trying to un-wrinkle the folds of a Chicago map back to a semblance of order.

You know there are only seven people on our planet who can make a paper map fit well enough to comfortably hibernate in a gloveless glovebox. You know, *you know* that you *wanted to know*, how many folks, the cranky, sanguinary editor killed. The voyage to the film's conclusion, will have to wait.

You hope the killer got the girl who hung out by the Bunn coffee machine and giggled in a muddled goofy manner when the high school football reporter was found dead in his car, in the drive-through lane of the Burger King. He never got his Whopper with Cheese.

His end created an awkward traffic jam.

You wish you could just quiver your head and whoosh this garbage away. But at least it's late. The rubbage has found a comfortable, easy chair, in the living room of your cranium.

You're back to the hallway. You can't recall ever walking down the hallway with the Swiffer because you can't find bags to fit your aging Kirby vacuum. The idle Kirby just collects dust. You look at your fingers, and realize your skin cells are flaking off and creating the dust.

You are the problem.

You glance. The creative part of your mind, *and you do mind,* are manufacturing hungry gargoyles in the room at the end of the hall at the south end of your flat. Your head's activity doesn't stand at attention as you slap it about. Now, the gargoyles show meat-eating, wisdom teeth.

How come, there can't be friendly gargoyles?

You could ask the cat, if he or she, would carefully walk down the hallway, and make sure safety exists, "Hey, Cat, would you…could you do a guy a favor?"

The cat stares at your gut. He, or she realizes that he, or she, is completely dependent on you. You buy the Fancy Feast food, for 79 cents a meal. You provide clean water. You clean up cat poops. You don't say anything rude because you don't even know the cat's sex. This is the first time you ever asked the cat for dispensation. The cat does, after all, tolerate your existence.

It really isn't your flat after all. You just pay the rent, and utilities. You have come to the realization, that you exist to feed the cat. You can ask the cat anything, but you may as well ask the Kirby, for favors. The cat leaps off the loveseat toward the hallway. Your heart has a second of satisfaction. The cat turns around, and comes back into the room, and perches on the windowsill.

It stares out.

You're disappointed in the cat. You should really get around to naming the cat, but you just can't get to it. The TV blares a snowy screen. Your heart still races from the video drama. You can't get it out of your head, that there probably aren't too many newspaper editors who have *KILL KILL KILL* wallpapered to the living room walls inside their heads.

You try not to freak out, when you hear Marlene, and Palmer Malone, your lovely upstairs neighbors enjoying intercourse right above you. You know from audio-experience, their mattress springs could use more than a little WD40 that their intercourse sessions last less than four minutes. It's an excused interruption. It always ends with Palmer yelping out, "Smoking." You assume they resume their mission of filling the Miller Park Zoo ashtray with Pall Mall butts after their late autumn delight.

You could sleep on your loveseat. Your shoes are already off. So you are, in essence, *ready for bed*. You have found, over the years, that as long as the shoes are history, sleep can creep up at any moment.

You shouldn't fear, but you do.

The VCR tape shouldn't have stirred up *shit,* but it has. You can't get around that. You certainly are big enough to whoop somebody's body part. But it's been forty years, since you punched Tom Rotramel's face with big mittens on your hands, at the bike rack of the Franklin Jr. High School. He hit you in the head, with a snowball. Kids gathered around you and Tom, chanting the obvious, "Fight, Fight, Fight!"

You stopped hitting Rotramel, after Mr. Glasgow, the science teacher, hollered out a window, "Desist that activity."

You did.

You don't hear people use the *desist* word anymore.

So, no fights since 7th grade. You still feel victorious, because of your triumph over Rotramel. You could still bring it on. You might still bring it on. You walk down the hall.

A dresser drawer is half open. Something is crawling out. Is it a long, lively sock? Is it a boa constrictor, camped in an argyle environment? You lose whatever swagger you had. You fall. *Prone—you sneak a look at your attacker. The demon* is a Levi's leg that has awakened and decided that today is the day to *BE.*

You will be the first Methodist, to get strangled by a demon leg. You crouch on all fours.

The cat!

The cat jumps on your back! Then pounces on the pant leg. And whatever life the pants had is gone.

You stand. Turn on the lights. Do a gargoyle search, and find none.

Everything is cool.

Right there, you name the cat…

"Trousers."

Watermelon

There was air in them bike tires.

Air was still free at the gas station, across the street from Steak n' Shake.

John spit a honker on the ground.

I got on the blue bike; he got on the red one.

We bought into the quick, air blowing freedoms in our faces.

We headed north on 51, into the pronouncement of Normal.

We swerved around vehicles waiting for Big Macs; we stopped at a liquor store.

John went inside, and bought himself a child's sized bottle of bourbon.

I got a Milky Way.

I followed him.

I felt like we were flying.

Whatever it was that pushed one's foot to pedal, was our precious zeal.

We entered our university.

We dashed between students.

We rode on the quad's grass.

We shifted gears.

We made these moments count, as high as an Illinois State University student could count anyway.

We zoomed like young men zoom.

He began doing a circle around Stevenson Hall and Waterson Towers, I followed his loop.

Then he started singing the Watermelon song.

He sang that song, when he was happy.

So, I sang too. "Water, water, water, melon, melon, melon," and on, and on.

We did it loud and clear.

Enunciating a clearly joyful produce cheer.